The Roman Riddle

A 1920s historical mystery

A Dora and Rex Mystery
Book 5

Lynn Morrison

Marketing Chair Press

Cover design by DLR Cover Designs

Published by

The Marketing Chair Press, Oxford, England

LynnMorrisonWriter.com

Print ISBN: 978-1-7392632-6-3

Contents

Chapter 1
Yet Another Castle

F laming torches cast flickering shadows on the narrow drawbridge. They danced left and right, shifting like expert swordsmen in the heat of battle.

Ahead, an arched entrance beckoned passersby to enter the thick stone walls. Royals and peasants alike had found safety within their embrace. The narrow slits carved into the stone promised to rain fiery arrows on any foe.

Tonight, however, there was no threat of being cut down. Strains of violins and a hum of voices proclaimed the gathering a peaceful one.

Still, Rex felt a shiver run along his spine. Another assignment in another castle.

This time, at least, he wasn't in England.

The crenelated parapet of Scaligero Castle in Sirmione, Italy, towered above Rex's head. Set on the southern end of Lake Garda, along a narrow peninsula jutting into the freshwater waves, Sirmione was a far cry from the rolling hills of Windsor. The historic fortress was the site of tonight's event — an open air ball to celebrate its recent restoration.

Instead of the crisp vowels of the English upperclass, the voices around Rex flowed in the singsong patter of the Italian language. Even the lake air held a distinct scent, tinged with notes of tomatoes and herbs from the nearby trattoria.

Only two things remained unchanged — the friend at his back and the woman on his arm.

Lord Clark, the friend in question, gave a narrow-eyed gaze to the dark moat waters that flowed under the stone bridge. His brow furrowed in concern. "Should my baser instincts overcome my good intentions, promise you won't let me go for a swim."

Rex shuddered at the thought. Although the spring night was warm enough to avoid the necessity of an overcoat, it was far too cool for a dip in the lake.

Theodora Laurent, Rex's paramour and partner-in-spying, shook her red-gold curls at the both of them. She reached up to tweak his moustache. "Come now, Clark. You've displayed nothing but excellent behaviour for the past four months. What makes you believe tonight will be any different?"

Clark opened his arms wide, gesturing at the people filling the piazza in front of the castle entrance. "Have you looked around, Theodora? Gone are the staid Swiss and stuffy French with whom we spent the prior months. Here in Italy, land of the dolce vita, resolutions are powerless against the bold red wine filling our glasses. I fear my resolve will come out the loser." To emphasise his point, Clark covered his face with his hand.

Dora slid free from Rex and hurried to Clark's side. She patted his arm. "Stick close to me and I'll teach you the art of sipping instead of gulping. It is an excellent way to indulge while still keeping your wits."

Clark flashed her a grateful smile. The receiving line shifted forward, allowing their group to enter the castle proper. Rex watched as Clark and Dora went ahead, leaning close together and then laughing over some shared joke.

He had no cause to be jealous. In a secret ceremony, witnessed only by a select few, he and Dora had pledged their troth. Although the rest of the world remained clueless, in the privacy of their home, they referred to one another as husband and wife.

Wedding rings were, of course, out of the question. Dora, however, had found a way to show her commitment, even if no one else understood. Already, her habit of wearing circular pendants and interwoven chains had started a new trend. She'd gifted Rex with a custom-designed Swiss watch, complete with a diamond-encrusted circle framing the watch face. He wore it proudly, not for the monetary value, but for the sentimental reason behind it.

The ticking hands on the watch face urged him to move forward. Inside, more torches graced the stone walls surrounding the central courtyard. Unlike Windsor, Scaligero Castle lacked the lavish interiors Rex usually associated with royalty. Since the fourteenth century, it had served as a fortress and fortified port. Watchmen had once stood sentinel in its tall towers, keeping watch against outside threats.

Tonight, however, the rich and beautiful were the only people parading around the parapet. Instead of knights in armour, a string quartet occupied the balcony. Under the covered walkways, waiters in black suits circulated with trays, offering prosecco and antipasti to the guests.

Rex caught sight of Dora's gleaming bob. Arm-in-arm with Clark, she was making a beeline for Gabriele D'Annunzio. A hero of the Great War turned literati, the man was always surrounded by a crowd of fawning men and women. He could be depended upon to foster debate and heated opinion.

Despite their evening finery and cavalier attitudes, Rex and Dora had business on their minds. Mussolini's hold on Italy's government strengthened by the day. Lord Audley, England's preeminent spy master, had sent the pair to Italy to gather information. To the outside world, Mussolini had a reputation for being fierce, often showing a willingness to use violence and threats to achieve his goals. Lord Audley wanted to know what Italian people really thought of the man. He trusted Dora, Rex, and their household of trained associates, to ferret out the truth.

Tonight, far from the reach of Rome, was an excellent chance for them to ask pointed questions. Rex felt no need to add to the numbers around D'Annunzio. Therefore, he left Dora and Clark on their own and turned his attention to the other guests.

Rex scanned the courtyard, searching for a familiar face. He was perfectly capable of starting a conversation with a stranger. But here, everyone was speaking in Italian.

Dora had assured him his language skills were up to snuff. To prove her point, they'd dressed in simple clothing and wandered the market, playing the role of tourists. The locals had embraced his halting attempts with open arms. To them, finding any Englishmen who made an effort to learn their language was enough. Still, the party attendees were from a different stratosphere — intellectuals, politicians, and the wealthy. Would they think him charming or ridiculous? He was unsure, and that caused him to hesitate.

He tossed a glance in Dora's direction. She was wedged between Clark and D'Annunzio. The trio smiled for a photographer. Dora flashed her white teeth, to cover for the calculating glint in her eyes.

Rex doubted the photo was an accident. What better way to hide her commitment to him? When the photo ended up on the society pages, her reputation as a femme fatale would remain intact.

"Pity that, isn't it?"

Rex turned at the feminine voice to find a dark-haired beauty at his side. She, too, stared at the trio, but with her wide lips turned down in a frown.

"Sorry?" Rex asked. He glanced around, wondering if she was talking to someone else.

She met his eyes, erasing any doubts.

"Have we met?"

The woman shook her head, allowing her diamond earrings to catch the light. She was of a similar height to Dora, but her hair as dark as her eyes, and her shape was more voluptuous. She tossed back the last of her prosecco and handed the glass to a server.

"I am Silvia and you are Lord Rex." She offered a bejewelled hand for him to kiss. "Now we are introduced. We might as well become acquainted, as it seems we are destined to end the night alone."

Rex knew a litany of acceptable ways to reply to an introduction, but none of them fit. Instead, he blurted out the first thing that came to mind. "What do you mean?"

Silvia pointed toward Dora. "She arrived on your arm, but she will leave on one of theirs. Likely Gabriele," she muttered. "Who can resist his genius?"

Rex could think of a few people, himself included, but he kept that to himself. The Italian woman was still talking.

"To think he almost died last year. Now he is here, so close to my home. It is a sign that I must pursue a relationship with him, but he hardly pays me notice. Especially not with her around." She spit out the last few words while glaring daggers at Dora.

As though the weight and heat of Silvia's gaze had attracted his attention, at that moment D'Annunzio glanced their way. His eyes narrowed at the sight of them.

"Ecco la! La gelosia!" Silvia cooed in delight.

Rex didn't need a translator to know what she'd said. *Jealousy.*

She snapped her fingers to call the photographer over. Without a word, she sidled closer to Rex, laying a hand over his chest. The flash from the camera left him seeing spots.

Silvia took further advantage of his discombobulation. She rose onto her toes and bussed him on the cheek. "Piacere, Lord Rex. Molto piacere. Thanks to your help, perhaps I won't go home alone after all."

With that, she slipped away as silently as she had arrived. She hurried over to D'Annunzio's side and kissed his cheeks in a hello.

Rex abandoned all plans to gather information. Instead, he helped himself to a glass of deep red Valpolicella and headed for the nearest staircase. He climbed to the next level and approached the far wall. He pulled the fresh night air into his lungs while letting his gaze wander along the moonlit waters of Lake Garda.

The Italians were so different from the British. None of the stiff upper lip. Every emotion rolled across their faces like the lapping waves of the lake waters. Their hands flew like the gulls circling overhead. They were friendly and passionate, as quick to let their tempers flare as to shower someone with praise. Rex had trouble keeping his balance as the emotions flowed around him. He'd discovered that a few minutes on his own was the best defence when he was overwhelmed.

After playing the pawn in Silvia's game of emotional chess, he needed a moment.

But it was not to be. The scuff of a shoe alerted him to the arrival of someone else. He didn't need to turn to know their identity.

Dora slid her arm around his back and rested her head on

his shoulder. "Gabriele had much to say about Mussolini, but held his tongue because of the crowd. He's invited us to visit his home tomorrow."

"Us or you?" Rex asked.

"Does it matter?" she replied. "Where one goes, the other follows. Forever," she added in a whisper.

Rex turned his head. Dora tilted hers until their lips met.

An abrupt cough interrupted them before they got too far. Rex looked back to see a young man dressed in a dark blue uniform, standing there with his cap under his arm.

"Scusate, ma, Lei é la Signora Laurent?"

Dora nodded. "I am," she replied in flawless Italian.

The young man stammered an explanation in an Italian so rapid, Rex could not keep up. Then he handed Dora a folded paper.

"What is it?" Rex asked.

"A telegram. An urgent one. He's been told to await a reply." She unfolded the paper, her eyes opening wider as she skimmed the short lines of text.

Rex's stomach clenched. "What is it? Is it Grandmama? Your family?"

Although, why would any of them send a message to her and not to him?

Dora read the page again, as though she needed a second time to process the words. Then, without answering Rex, she looked at the waiting man. "Veniamo subito. Questa é la risposta."

The man bobbed his head and disappeared down the stairs.

That, at least, had been simple enough for Rex to understand.

"Go where? Now?" Rex pelted Dora with questions, too worried to phrase them as complete sentences.

Dora folded the note and tucked it into the top of her dress.

Only then did she turn her wide-eyed gaze up to meet Rex's worried one. She grabbed onto his lapels and tugged him close until she could whisper in his ear.

"We're needed in Rome. The British Ambassador has been accused of murder."

Chapter 2
Rome's Call for Help

Leaving an event so early without attracting too much attention was easier said than done. Dora suggested they split up. Rex would go first. He set off to watch for a crowd of arrivals and then slide out the front while everyone was distracted. In the shadows of the piazza, he'd wait for Dora to catch up.

Meanwhile, Dora returned to the party, this time with only a weak smile for those she passed. She made her way to Clark and waited until she could extract him from the group. With raised eyebrows, he followed her to a nearby alcove.

"Darling, I hate to be a wet blanket on this wonderful evening, but Rex and I must duck out. We need you to make our excuses."

Clark's expression shifted. "Is anything amiss? Of course it is," he added, answering himself.

Dora grinned. "I received an urgent telegram from a friend in Rome and simply must dash to their aid."

At this, Clark's concern cleared. "You are ever so good in a crisis. I can see why they'd ask for your help. What do you need me to do?"

"First, please tell anyone who asks that I've come down with something and Rex escorted me home. Stay as long as you'd like. Tomorrow, can you make your way to Rome with the others? I hate to cut our stay here short, but from what little I know, this is likely to require all hands on deck."

Clark drew himself up and adopted a military stance. For all his love of shenanigans, he proved to be most excellent in a time of need. Well, so long as he wasn't at the centre of said crisis.

This time, he stood most certainly on the periphery. Dora had complete confidence he would do as she asked.

He mimed a salute. "I'll get away as soon as I can. You can count on me for whatever help you need with the arrangements."

Dora kept her head down as she left, doing her level best to convince everyone she felt poorly. Together, she and Rex hurried along the main street to their rented accommodation. It was so close they hadn't bothered with the car.

They walked in to find Inga and Harris waiting in the foyer. Their dear friends were not surprised by their early return.

"You told the messenger where he could find me?" Dora confirmed as she shrugged off her wrap.

"When he expressed the need for an immediate response, I believed it was the most appropriate course of action. Was the message from Lord Audley?"

"Strangely, no. It was from Rome — from the British ambassador."

Inga drew up short. "Really! How on earth did he learn you are here?"

"That will be the second question I ask. Rex and I must leave for Rome at first light. Can you spare Archie to drive us? We'll leave Basil and Cynthia behind to help you pack."

Inga nodded at Harris, and he bolted off to find Archie.

"Now that we've settled that, could we return to our earlier point? You said how he found you would be your second question for the ambassador. What, pray tell, will be the first?"

"Who is he accused of murdering?"

Inga gasped. Even she, with her formidable intelligence, hadn't foreseen that answer. "I imagine many more questions will follow that one. While you get changed, I'll prepare some food and coffee. Moving a household of our size on a moment's notice requires a well-laid plan."

"How soon will you be able to follow?"

Inga tapped her chin. "Assuming I can get someone to assist me in the train office on a Sunday, we should make it to Rome by Monday evening."

Dora would not do better than that. She and Rex went upstairs, changed into travelling clothes, and each packed an overnight case. They turned in early, for them anyway. When the sun rose on Sunday morning, Archie took his place behind the wheel, and set off toward Verona. From there, they assumed it would be easy enough to get to Rome.

A flat tyre outside of Florence threw their schedule into disarray. With the repair shop closed until morning, the three had to stay in a hotel overnight. Thus, it was Monday afternoon by the time they crossed into the outskirts of Rome.

In the motorcar's backseat, Dora sighed in relief when the road signs indicated they were near their destination. The endless hours of riding had her head full of cobwebs. She rubbed her eyes and then stretched her arms wide in a yawn.

Her rustling caught Rex's ear. He turned around and passed her their thermos. "I saved the last bit of water for you. We're almost there, yet I am still in the dark about your connection to the ambassador. How well are you acquainted with him? Is there anything specific I should know?"

Dora had hoped to avoid this conversation, even though she'd been expecting it. She wasn't entirely sure she trusted her judgement when it came to the man. "I met him during my last visit, and I can't say we grew particularly close. Suffice it to say that I helped him through a difficult time."

"Care to elaborate on any of that?"

"Not yet. I'd prefer you form your own opinion before I tell you anything that might colour it."

In the front seat, Rex and Archie exchanged confused glances, neither knowing what to make of her answer.

Dora refused to be drawn out further. The truth was that she had no idea what to make of the situation. Nor could she guess whether Lord Audley was involved.

Archie's grip on the steering wheel tightened as they approached the centre of Rome. Despite having braved the roads of London, Paris, and Geneva during their spring travels, he was wholly unprepared for the chaos of the Eternal City. Cars, buses, bicycles, and pedestrians fought for space on the old roads and pavements. Painted lines and street signs were treated as suggestions at best. The more imaginative ignored them all, simply riding wherever their eyes spotted a gap.

And yet, somehow, it all worked. Rome's inhabitants moved in an elaborately choreographed dance, as if guided by an invisible hand. Perhaps that was what gave Archie the confidence to raise his gaze from the road and look around.

He pointed to a familiar shape on the skyline. "Is that?"

"The Colosseum," Dora confirmed. The stone walls dominated their view on the left. For nearly two thousand years, the imposing facade with its lines of arched openings had stood as a testament to the once great empire. "Up ahead is the Roman Forum, or what is left of it, anyway. You'll have plenty of time to explore."

"Blimey! " Archie gaped at the skyline. In his distraction, he lifted his foot from the accelerator.

Rex patted the man on his shoulder. "An accurate, if brief, description. Although this is my second visit, the Colosseum never fails to impress."

A blaring horn urged them onward. Dora gave Archie instructions to where the ambassador lived. Given the hour and the circumstances, she was betting they'd find him at home.

His Roman villa befit his status. A thick stucco wall encircled the grounds. Tall umbrella palms and thick hedges blocked the house from view. The flag flying near the front gate proclaimed its ownership.

An armed guard stood sentry. That was new. The ambassador had not exaggerated his risk. After verifying their names against their list of permitted visitors, they waved the trio ahead.

Archie drove to the front of the house and stopped the car.

"Wait here," Dora instructed. "I don't intend to stay long."

"Are we not here to help him?" Rex murmured.

"We will," Dora replied. "But if it is a murder we must solve, I doubt we'll find the answer in there. Let's get the lay of the land and then excuse ourselves to regroup with the others."

Archie bobbed his head and reached into his pack for the last of Inga's wrapped sandwiches. Dora and Rex exited the car.

Dora stood still and gazed upon the house, looking for any changes or signs that things were amiss. Strangely, the exterior exactly matched the picture in her mind's eye. Like much of Rome, it resisted the march of time.

It was not, however, impervious to threats.

The front door opened, and a perfectly dressed English butler stepped out to welcome them. His thick, white hair was so slicked back with pomade that it didn't move. He held himself perfectly still, positioned at the door like a stone soldier guarding his liege for all eternity.

Dora circled the car and offered Rex her hand. Together, they closed the distance.

The butler unbent enough to execute a bow. "Good afternoon, Lord Reginald and Miss Laurent. The ambassador is expecting you."

They entered the stately home with its cold, grey marble floors and curving staircase dominating the spacious entry. Marble busts looked upon them from their pedestals, while priceless works of art hung on the walls.

It was a home fit for a king, should his majesty ever choose to visit. In the interim, his appointed representative retained occupancy.

That wasn't the only connection between the ambassador and the royal family. Sir Francis Cannon was twenty-fifth in line for the throne. He had only an infinitesimal chance of inheriting the crown, but you'd never know by the way he told it. In England, members of the aristocracy rolled their eyes. Only abroad did anyone give weight to his exaggerations.

The butler showed them to a small parlour. Sir Francis was already there with a drink in hand. He leapt to his feet at their arrival and rushed to shake their hands.

"Oh, Theodora! You are a sight for my weary eyes. I half-feared you wouldn't come."

"I could hardly ignore such a desperate plea for help, Sir Francis. Neither I nor Lord Rex," Dora added, bringing Rex into the conversation.

She noted with satisfaction that Rex took time to survey the man and his surroundings. The room could have just as easily been in a London men's club, with its leather furniture, hunting paintings, filled bookshelves, and smell of cigars.

Sir Francis offered the pair a drink, but they both declined. This wasn't a social call.

After they took their seats, with Dora claiming the seat beside the ambassador and Rex sitting across from them, Sir Francis launched his tale.

"It's horrid, Theodora. Simply horrid. I don't understand how the Carabinieri can think I'm involved! What reason would I have to murder anyone? And me, a relative of King George!"

Dora worked overtime to keep any hint of judgement from her expression. "You poor dear! What has happened? Start from the beginning. Your telegram was the first word we had of the situation."

Sir Francis took a fortifying sip of his libation before doing as she asked. "It happened three nights ago. Someone murdered a woman, strangled her on the pavement outside the gates of my estate. I thought nothing of it at first. These things happen in major cities. Rome has its fair share of crime."

Dora hoped she'd never be so sanguine about the loss of life, even of a stranger. But she kept that to herself.

Rex cleared his throat. "Who was the woman? Was she one of the servants?"

"The papers published her photo. I'd never seen her before in my life." Sir Francis's hand shook, causing the ice in his glass to clink and sending a whiff of whiskey into the air.

Dora and Rex exchanged glances. Thus far, nothing the Ambassador said explained why he believed he was implicated. Rex gave Dora a nod of encouragement.

She bequeathed the ambassador with a sympathetic smile. "I'm sure this is a case of misinterpretation. Of course you were right to call upon us. We're happy to lend our moral support during this difficult time."

Sir Francis's head snapped up. "It isn't moral support I need. You must investigate! Prove my innocence!"

Dora rocked back at his vehement tone. "Why do you believe you will be charged? Proximity alone isn't a sign of guilt."

"Besides," Rex added, "you have diplomatic immunity. Even in the worst case scenario, you can return to England."

"Where my career and my reputation will be in tatters?" Sir Francis shook his head in a swift arc. "I have served the crown in various postings for most of my adult life. If I return, stained by a murder charge, I'll be consigned to the pasture with King George's Hereford stock."

His logic rang true. Dora herself had always taken great care to avoid the reach of the law. Public drunkenness might be overlooked. But murder? Theft? Her days as a spy would end.

That explained why he wanted to clear his name. But on the matter of alleged guilt, she still had many questions.

Rex's patience ran out. "Sir Francis, why do you think you are a suspect? Did you venture out on the night in question?"

Sir Francis turned his wild-eyed gaze in Rex's direction. "Not 'a' suspect. *The suspect.* The only one. The general in charge of the Carabinieri paid me a call with the news. He claimed he had inscrutable evidence that places me at the scene. He intends to petition Re Vittorio Emanuele for the right to arrest me."

His words made little sense... unless.

"Have you angered the king or Mussolini? Are they trying to rid themselves of you without angering the British government?"

"No!" Sir Francis threw his hands in the air. "Re Vittorio is a dear friend. And Mussolini has nothing to fear from me. I've not dirtied my hands with local matters."

"Someone wants you gone," Rex insisted. "Think, man!"

Sir Francis deflated and flopped against the back of the sofa. "I swear, since the General left, I've done nothing else. I reached out to others who are here. No one has a clue why this is happening. Even the Re himself. He agreed to give me time to clear my name — a brief window, not forever. I was desperate for help, but where to turn? Then, a guardian angel suggested the pair of you."

An angel? Dora had never heard Lord Audley described in such terms. A demon? Sure. But if he was behind any part of this, he'd have sent word. Dora suspected someone else must be involved. Faces flashed in her mind's eye. Her father? Benedict?

Sir Francis found his energy again. He stood and motioned for them to follow. "You must be exhausted. And, of course, she'll be expecting you." He froze, mid-step. "Oh, the Carabinieri! How can we convince them to speak to you?"

For this, at least, Dora had a solution. "Lord Clark Kenworthy is with us. He is a member of the House of Lords. Perhaps the embassy could issue him and Rex temporary credentials? He has already promised to lend a hand."

Sir Francis exhaled in sheer relief and started again for the door.

This time, Rex stopped him. "Before we go, I really must insist you tell us who gave you our names and our direction. We've been gone from England for months. We weren't due in Rome for another week."

Sir Francis glanced between Dora and Rex, his disbelief evident. "Why it was the Dowager Duchess of Rockingham, of course! Your grandmother," he added, looking at Rex. "She's been in Rome for several weeks. She arrived soon after Prince Albert and Princess Elizabeth's wedding."

Dora bit the inside of her cheek to keep from laughing. Rex was so flummoxed by the news his grandmother was in town that he stumbled into a chair.

Although Dora was caught equally unaware, she was far from shocked. She and Inga had placed bets on how long it would take someone from their families to catch up.

Dora's money had been on Benedict. Inga, however, had placed her bet on Edith. Inga would be insufferable as soon as she learned she'd won.

But Dora wasn't the only one who would have to pay up. Given the colour rising along Rex's neck, Dora doubted the dowager duchess was going to get off scot free.

Chapter 3
The Surprise Visitor

R ex restrained himself from slamming the car door but it
was a near thing. The flames of righteous indignation
burned the back of his throat. Fortunately for them all, Dora
had the presence of mind to ask for his grandmother's
whereabouts. She'd nodded at the address, seemingly familiar
with the neighbourhood.

That left Rex free to wonder what sort of game his
grandmother was playing. The cacophony of blaring horns
when Archie pulled the car into the traffic set Rex off.

"How dare my grandmother drag us into this! She knows
how hard we've had to work to keep our cover of aimless party-
goers. Putting on a show for the gossip columnists is pain
enough. Here in Italy, I wanted to be free of the weight of my
name. She's yoked me again."

"I'm sure Edith has her reasons," Dora murmured in a
soothing tone.

"Such as? I apologise for speaking out of turn, but the
ambassador's stance rubbed me the wrong way. His blithe
insouciance over a woman's death turned my stomach. The only
thing he cares about is his own hide."

Dora tsked. "Many would say the same about Clark, but that didn't make him guilty of Hugh's murder, no matter how the situation appeared at first glance."

Rex ignored her comments. He was in no mood to be talked down. It was best for all of them he let his anger burn bright now.

He hoped for a long ride through town to give him time to cool off. Instead, the journey from one doorstep to the other took less than ten minutes. All too soon, Dora pointed toward a narrow drive beside an impressive townhouse. Archie followed it to a rear courtyard and parked the car.

"We're here. If you can hold your tongue for a moment longer, you can tell your grandmother what you think to her face."

Rex's stomach clenched again. No one shouted at his grandmother and lived to tell the tale. Not even his father dared to tell her no.

Even should he opt to run headlong into such a foolhardy mistake, it would be for naught. His grandmother was as intractable as the Roman emperors of old.

Cold rationale poured over the flames of his anger, dashing them as effectively as a pail of water. "I'll remain civil, but only until she has given us an explanation. If it isn't up to snuff, I retain the right to share my thoughts on her actions."

"Of course, darling," Dora purred. She patted his arm. "Now you know how poor Lord Audley must feel when you and I sow the seeds of chaos in our efforts to accomplish something good."

Despite her calming tone, Dora's words did little to mollify Rex. Still, he allowed her to accompany him around the side of the house to the front door.

His grandmother's butler, Sheffield answered the door. His sedate expression didn't shift at finding them on the doorstep.

"Master Reginald, Miss Laurent, welcome to Rome." He

stood aside and motioned for them to enter. He led them into a spacious reception room with high ceilings and narrow windows.

The home was a rental, furnished in a style appropriate for the warmer Mediterranean climate. Similarly, his grandmother wore a flowing silk dress in a becoming shade of lavender. She smiled beatifically at the pair as they entered.

"Oh good, you made it. Sheffield, please see to some refreshments for Rex and Theodora? They must be parched after their long drive." She waved them to take a seat.

Rex's ire rose once again. Did she truly intend to act as though they'd popped in for a social call?

"I take it you visited Sir Francis first?"

He choked back his initial response, opting for something closer to civil. "Given we remained unaware of your presence in town, we could hardly do otherwise, Grandmama."

"And yet, you've found me. Your decision to come over straightaway was excellent, as I have much on which to update you." When Rex's forehead wrinkled, she added, "Surely you didn't assume I'd acted rashly."

Dora laid a hand on his arm. "I told you, darling. Edith has her reasons. I suggest we let her tell us why we're really here."

Edith gave Dora a nod of thanks. Rex slumped in the nearest chair, sitting like a sullen child. He was abroad, hundreds of miles from home, and married. And yet, he was still under his grandmother's thumb. Dora sat beside him and nudged him to sit up straight. He complied, but did little to adjust his attitude.

The butler arrived, carrying a tray of tall glasses filled with a pale liquid. The lemon slices floating inside proclaimed it to be lemonade. One sip of the tart liquid made his mouth pucker, but the sweet aftertaste beckoned him back.

"Divine, isn't it? The lemons are from Sicily," his grandmother explained.

Dora took a sip, murmured her compliments, and then set the drink aside. "You were about to tell us why you told the ambassador to request our help."

"The moment I saw the woman's photograph in the newspaper, I knew something was afoot. Killed outside the ambassador's home in the dead of night? That smacked of intrigue. I sent a telegram to Lord Audley. He said I should send for you."

That answered one of Rex's questions. "In that case, how is it that Sir Francis sent the message?"

"The poor man rang. He was a mess. Said the police had visited, issuing threats. Given my stature in society, he asked if I'd speak on his behalf. I saw an opportunity to make your lives easier. I mentioned how you two had helped Bertie with a spot of bother earlier in the year. He knew Dora, of course, and immediately took to the idea."

"Why didn't you ring us then?" Rex asked in consternation.

"I had to let it play out, you see. It wouldn't do for Sir Francis to think I was pulling his strings." She beamed at Dora and Rex.

Rex stared at his grandmother. Her story was so full of holes as to be nearly transparent. Surely she didn't mean to end there.

But she carried on smiling, motioning for them to taste the canapés.

"Grandmama!" Rex groused, having reached the limits of his patience. "Why are you in Rome? Why did you immediately suspect treachery? How did you know we were in Sirmione? And what about my cat? I left Mews in your care."

A delicate v formed between her eyebrows. "Rex dear, you've hardly travelled incognito. Not a week goes by without your names showing up in the society pages. I looked at your route thus far, put two and two together, and landed upon Lake Garda. Anyone could have guessed that Dora would want to visit D'Annunzio. Was I wrong? Don't answer that. Your presence here is proof enough."

"And your presence?" he asked.

"I came for my own purposes, which have nothing to do with you. As for Mews, he is being well cared for by my housekeeper." Her glare dared him to ask for more.

Rex chose to stay in the shallow waters. Her pique, once risen, could drown a man.

"The treachery? Did you know the woman? The victim?" he clarified.

"Like Sir Francis, I'd never seen her before." She flattened her lips into a straight line.

Dora leaned forward, just as struck by Edith's body language. "Someone knew her. Someone close to you... Convincing enough to make you confident in your assessment of the situation. Was the victim stepping out with the footman?"

Edith shifted in her chair.

"Come now, Edith," Dora cajoled. "Surely there mustn't be any secrets between us at this point. Not if we're meant to investigate."

"The woman had visited here a week earlier. She tuned the piano in the music room."

Rex threw caution to the mind. He was done playing this game. "Shall I call for Sheffield? Question the servants?"

"Pish posh, Rex. You act as though I am some kind of criminal. If you'll settle down, I'll explain."

Rex gave her a dry look. He was unamused.

"As I was saying, the woman worked as a piano tuner. A rather good one, or so I'm told. We hired her through a local firm, and she introduced herself with an Italian surname. She spoke English, but with a heavy accent. She completed her task, left, and was dead within a week."

"Did she tune the ambassador's piano? If so, that is hardly a smoking gun."

"The young lady was English, Rex. As English as the three of us. Her accent was fake. Her name, likely fake as well."

Rex parsed through her words, searching for what had gone unsaid. His grandmother had no reason to be here, and little enough love of the piano.

But someone else in his family had a well-known passion for the instrument's ivory keys. Rex pictured a young girl, before realising that was wrong. His sister was a woman now. "Caledonia is here?"

"Rex's sister?" Dora asked. She tossed a frantic glance at the doorway. "She's here? Now?"

Rex understood her concern. Dora had yet to meet the rest of his family. Rex was still mulling over the best way to tell them about their marriage.

These were hardly the ideal circumstances for them to meet. Here, in Rome, with no preparation.

Rex hadn't seen her in ages. What to say? And how to explain his involvement in a murder investigation.

Wait a moment...

"Caledonia has a connection to the victim? Dear Lord, don't tell me they were friends!"

"Caledonia was not acquainted with her. However, the musical world is small. Their paths had crossed before - in England," his grandmother added. "When Caledonia read the news, she was caught off guard by the victim's name. She was certain the woman was not Italian. There is more happening than what appears on the surface. How far and how deep the problem goes will be for you to discover. I've done my part by getting you here."

Edith crossed her hands on her lap and adopted her famous upright stance.

Rex released a deep-seated sigh. Much as he wanted to chastise his grandmama, he found no fault with her actions. He let go of any thoughts of carrying on with further recriminations. There were more important matters left to discuss.

"I'll need to speak with Callie," he said, using his sister's childhood nickname. "Then you must take her home."

"I'll do no such thing. We are in Rome for our own reasons, as I already stated. Caledonia is studying with a maestro. You can't think to deny her this chance!"

Dora remained silent, choosing to stay out of the family matter.

"If someone, or worse yet, a group of someones are intent on taking down the British ambassador, then this is hardly a safe place for either of you," Rex insisted. He turned to Dora. "You explain it to her."

"There is nothing to explain. I am not a child. Neither is Caledonia. You two will sort this out in ample time to prevent any misfortune from befalling us. Now, I suggest you go to your home and rest. I'll expect you back for supper. Caledonia will return from her lesson by then. It will be an excellent opportunity for the two of you to reconnect."

"I agree," Dora said. She leapt to her feet and turned to face him. "We should make time for you to speak with her on your own. Edith, might Inga and I interest you in a game of cards after dinner?"

"Only if it is poker. I've been working on my bluffing abilities."

Rex's gaze pinged left and right, shifting between his grandmother and his wife. When had he relinquished all control over his decisions to them?

He didn't bother to voice the question. The women would most likely tell him he was fortunate to have them.

And he was. Of that, there could be no doubt. But just once, he'd like to be the one holding the reins.

There was still the conversation with his sister to be had. There, at least, he stood on solid ground. He was, after all, the older brother.

Chapter 4
Dora Recounts the Past

Dora did not raise the matter of Rex's younger sister during the drive to their temporary home. The brief hop didn't allow enough time to wade into such a significant topic.

Rex sat facing forward, but she doubted he took in any of the sites. The furrow in his brow and slack gaze suggested he needed time to gather his wits.

Caledonia's presence wasn't necessarily a bad thing. Rex had spoken once or twice about his desire to foster a stronger connection with his family. Each time, she'd pointed out that his grandmother was one of their most ardent supporters.

Eventually, she'd promised herself, he'd find the right occasion. Neither of them had foreseen how soon it would come.

Dora sensed Edith's invisible hand working behind the scene. It was only natural that Edith would want the rest of the family to get to know her. She was, after all, Rex's wife. Unfortunately, if Dora and Rex truly wanted a relationship with his family, there was no way to reveal that truth without hinting at the other secrets.

She'd give Rex time to digest the news before asking how he

wanted to handle her introduction. For now, the simplest course was to stick to their cover story. There wasn't any need to reveal everything on day one.

Right?

The little voice in the back of her mind piped up. It pointed out the troubles she'd caused by keeping things from her brother.

She did her level best to ignore that voice. Caledonia was a young woman, not a grown man.

Like you once were, the little voice reminded.

Fortunately, they arrived at their home before her conscience forced her to endure more hard truths.

She had arranged accommodation for their party at a large property near the Pantheon, a place she considered one of her homes away from home. It had six spacious bedroom suites, offering room enough for them all. The only hitch had come from Dora's staff. Her maid, Cynthia, and her twin brothers, Archie and Basil, had balked at the idea of living side-by-side with their employer.

Inga came through with a better solution, reminding Dora about the guesthouse in the garden. The guest house was just as nicely furnished, but far enough from the main house to remove any sense of obligation to serve. They'd be free to come and go as they pleased.

Dora put up no argument. She did, however, highlight that Rome was to be an educational visit for all of them. Instead of waiting on her, she wanted them to get out and see the world. They were to talk to locals and experience life in a foreign culture.

Archie stopped the car in front of the house and awaited further instruction. "Shall I bring the bags?"

"No, you shall not," Dora replied. "You are on holiday. If you pull the car around to the back, you'll find the guest house.

I'll ask Nonna Matilda to send someone to show you the place."

"Nonna Matilda? Is she a relative?"

"Not in the traditional sense. She is the housekeeper. Once you set foot in her home, you are forever part of her family."

Dora raised a hand to ring the doorbell, but Nonna Matilda opened it before she could do so. Short, round, and smelling of cinnamon and almonds, the old woman broke into a beatific smile at the sight of Dora and bundled her into an embrace.

"Cara Mia, Teodora!" she sang. She paused long enough to kiss both cheeks and then let her go. "Ma, che bella che sei! Sempre un sole!"

"No, Nonna Matilda, it is you who is the sun. We all revolve around you. At best, I am a stella twinkling in the sky."

Nonna Matilda patted Dora on the cheek and finally turned her gaze on Rex. "É lui?"

"Yes, this is him." Dora looked at Rex. "Darling, this is Nonna Matilda. She watched after me and Inga the last time we visited. She makes the best cannoli in Rome, but heaven help you if she catches you stealing one."

Nonna Matilda smacked Dora's hand and shook her head. "Ignore her. You are too pale and too skinny. For you, I will make pasta alla norma and all the dolcetti you can eat."

Dora let Nonna Matilda lead Rex inside. She noted a serving boy lingering in the corner and sent him to help Archie with the bags.

She kept quiet as the housekeeper rattled off dish after dish she'd already prepared. It made no difference that Rex's grandmother expected them for dinner. In this house, Matilda was in charge. And she had determined that they must eat.

Dora trusted her implicitly and loved her as though she were truly her grandmother. Matilda had been part of Lord Audley's network for years. In addition to a handful of servants, she also had access to a bevy of men and women who operated on the shadier side of the law. Such connections were vital to visiting spies who might have need of a deft pickpocket or talented thief.

Dora never asked where Matilda got the money for such an elegant villa. With four reception rooms, a large study, dining room, breakfast room, and a terrace into the garden, it ranked as one of the more impressive homes in Rome.

Matilda relented long enough to allow them to change clothes. Then, in her kitchen, she handed them plates filled with tempting delights. They barely got a bite before the rest of their crew arrived. Coming up from the rear of the house, Inga and Harris rapped on the kitchen door to get their attention.

Matilda threw open the door and pulled Inga into a hug, the two women squeezing each other extra tight. Then Harris stepped forward. He bowed his head, showing Matilda the respect appropriate for a family member. Matilda studied him carefully, pausing at his flamboyant pocket square and again at his Italian loafers.

She leaned close to Inga and muttered in Italian, "He is mischievous, no? A clown, but with a good heart?"

"That's a fair summation," Inga replied.

"Good. You are wound too tight. He will cause you to loosen up." Matilda then welcomed Harris with open arms.

Dora and Rex watched all this from their seats at the kitchen table. When no one else followed Harris in, Dora raised a question.

"Did you lose Clark?"

"Yes, at the train station," Inga answered. She hurried to add, "On purpose, mind you. He ran into someone he knew on the train. I suggested he go for a drink to see if he could learn who else was in town. He'll catch up shortly."

Relief buzzed through Dora at learning Clark hadn't got

into trouble. He'd turned over a new leaf, but the siren call of adventure was hard to ignore.

Nonna Matilda directed Inga and Harris upstairs, instructing them to come back down after washing the travel dust from their hands and faces. The enticing smells of the kitchen provided reason enough for them to hurry.

Over cups of espresso and plates of cannoli and tiny amaretti, Dora told Inga and Harris what they'd learned.

When she finished, Rex asked, "Now that we're all caught up, will you finally deign to tell us about the last time you saw the ambassador?"

Nonna Matilda pulled a silver tray from a cupboard. She loaded the plates of treats onto it and motioned for them to follow. "Go sit on the terrace and enjoy the spring air. I have much to clean up here and don't need you under foot."

They did as told, moving to a wrought-iron table with a glass top and four cushioned chairs. A faint breeze rustled the leaves and cooled their skin after the warm kitchen. Between the fresh air and strong coffee, they all found their second wind.

Dora began her story. "We were last in Rome three years ago. On an assignment, as you can imagine. We had received word that someone was leaking private information to the Italians, allowing them to get the upper-hand in negotiations. It was wide-ranging enough that only someone inside the embassy would have known."

"So you remained?" Rex asked.

"We had no choice. Alarm bells went off. Audley extended our mission. We were to stay until we uncovered the identity of the leak."

"It took us weeks," Inga said, picking up the thread. "As you'll see tomorrow, the embassy is a vast building, with many staff walking its halls. We had to be methodical, both of us working our way through the various possibilities. In the end, we narrowed our list to two suspects."

Harris reached for another amaretto biscuit. "Who were they?"

"Either the ambassador or his private secretary."

Rex and Harris both gaped. Harris recovered first. "I presume it was the latter, given the ambassador is still in his post."

"An easy guess," Dora said. "However, we can take no credit for solving the case."

"Huh?" Rex leaned forward. "Someone outsmarted you? Both of you?"

Dora flashed back to a wrinkled page written by an unsteady hand. "I wish that were the case. We must have done something- spoke to the wrong person. I don't know. Suffice it to say that the private secretary — a Mr Donald Tomlins — felt under pressure. Fearing he was about to be caught, he confessed everything in a note."

"A suicide note," Inga clarified. "The sentence for treason is death, but we both felt guilty over his untimely demise."

"He took his secrets to the grave. To make matters worse, we worried we'd blown our cover. I befriended the ambassador out of necessity, needing to know if he or anyone else had a clue about our involvement."

"That is why Sir Francis believes you to be friends?" Rex asked.

Dora nodded. "You have no idea how happy I was to leave by the end. I didn't like the man. In hindsight, I fear I let my opinion sway me in the wrong direction. Mr Tomlins was a friendly chap, always ready with a kind word. He didn't fit the picture of a traitor. But he was."

Quiet settled over the table as everyone reflected on the

story. Rex broke the silence. "What do you think this time around? What does your instinct say?"

Dora settled into a flat-lipped silence. She and Inga traded glances. Almost in unison, they shrugged their shoulders.

Dora forced her jaw to unlock. "As much as I'm loathe to admit this, I haven't a clue. Worse yet, I don't entirely trust my instincts. Last time, I was leaning toward the ambassador being guilty. It was easy to believe he'd sell his soul to gain riches. After all, his entire career is based upon some distant connection to the king."

"True, but he is also good at what he does," Inga reminded her. "England has never had an issue or miscommunication with any country while he was the ambassador. Even if he is a self-centred prat."

Harris snorted in surprise, and a vagrant laugh tore from Rex.

"That was my view as well," Rex conceded. "But as Dora said, that doesn't make him guilty. More likely, he angered the wrong person. Now, that someone is out to get him."

"But who?" Dora skimming her gaze around the table, studying her friends' faces. Unlike the clear skies above, their expressions were cloudy.

A booming baritone voice echoing from inside lifted their spirits. In short order, Nonna Matilda escorted Clark out to the terrace.

"I found this man on our doorstep. He claims to be a friend, but he turned down my offer of food." She scowled at Clark. "How good of a friend can he be if he doesn't know about Nonna Matilda's cooking skills?"

Clark read the looks of horror on their faces and blanched at his mistake. Then, in true Clark fashion, he set to work making things right. He dropped to one knee and clasped Matilda's hand in his.

"Signora, the only deficiency here is in my communication skills. I should have explained that I just ate. Your skills are legendary and deserve my full appetite and undivided attention. It would do you a disservice if I can do little more than nibble. Your meals are to be savoured."

Nonna Matilda flushed under his flurry of compliments. She lifted her free hand and patted him on the cheek. "You are right. Tomorrow, I will prepare a day-long feast, beginning with fresh-baked cornetti at breakfast and ending with an amaro at midnight. You will stay and eat."

"It would be my pleasure, signora," he pledged. He didn't stand up until she was safely back inside. "A little warning would have been nice," he grumbled to the group.

"Your mistake is our gain," Harris replied. "I don't know about the rest of you, but I'm looking forward to the feast."

"Save the food talk for tomorrow." Dora waited for Clark to bring over a chair. "What is the opinion of the masses? Has word of the ambassador's impending arrest got out?"

"It has, although I would not use the word masses to describe the social scene. Most of our countrymen returned north either to celebrate Bertie's nuptials or to flee the impending summer heat. The journalists, however, are here in force. Normally, I'd avoid them, but given the circumstances, I let my guard down. They were happy to give me the scoop on popular opinion."

"Do people think him guilty or innocent?"

"Split down the middle, I'm afraid."

Dora hadn't expected that answer. "What are the rationales for each position?"

"Half think him innocent for the same reason as we do. Why would Sir Francis be out, after dark, and with a stranger? That is hardly his style."

"And the rest?"

"The guilty voters are not focused on the Ambassador. Instead, they offer Mussolini as their explanation. The man is busy consolidating his control over the country. It makes no sense for him to risk angering the British. If the Carabinieri have his blessing to charge the ambassador, Mussolini must be convinced of his guilt."

Dora contemplated his explanation. "What of a motive?"

Clark shook his head. "None whatsoever. The only thing they agree upon is that it is fortunate his wife remained in England after the royal wedding. Most expect Lady Emily will wait until the hubbub passes before returning. This situation is likely giving her the vapours."

Rex glanced at Dora. "Could Sir Francis have been having an affair?"

Dora, Inga, and Clark all said no.

Dora explained, "Sir Francis's marriage was a love match. His wife, Lady Emily, is a dear friend of Queen Mary. There is no way he'd risk his marriage and his position on an untitled, unknown woman. I'm surprised no one raised a third possibility."

"What's that?" Clark asked.

"That the ambassador has been framed." Dora gazed at her friends, waiting for one of them to argue against the possibility. Instead, they were as stumped as she was.

A case with no motive, a victim with a fake identity, and the reputation of a senior political figure on the line. Based on what little she knew, this was likely to be the most challenging case of her life.

Although she was no stranger to difficult problems, this one had a twist. Last time, her instincts had led her astray. Would she do any better this go around?

Chapter 5
The Bond of Sisterhood

The car ride took an interminably long time. Every person in Rome was out in the streets, clogging the major thoroughfares with their automobiles and bicycles. Pedestrians had laid claim to the narrow side streets.

Rex fidgeted with the button on his suit jacket. He wiggled it from side to side, testing the limits of the thread holding it in place. His mind paid little attention to his hand. It was too busy preparing for the upcoming encounter with his little sister.

Dora reached over and laid a hand over his. "Stop worrying," she said, "if not for my sake, then on behalf of that innocent button."

Rex glanced on in horror to see the button hanging loose, the thread having stretched to the limits of its elasticity. "Bother!" he grumbled under his breath.

He and Dora had decided he should ease Caledonia into things. They'd give her time to get to know Dora before telling her about the seriousness of their commitment. It was the logical decision. Yet, for some unknown reason, Rex's stomach continued to roil.

Dora meant the world to him. He didn't mind keeping their

marriage from outsiders. But from his family? It felt like a double betrayal. Yet, her identity lay wrapped under layers of secrets, lies, and misdirection. That would take time to unpick.

Rex lifted Dora's hand and kissed her fingers. Tonight would be the first step in building a relationship with Caledonia- the first for both of them.

Dora looked impossibly elegant in a floor-length satin gown. She'd eschewed her normal vibrant colours for a pale green that drew attention to her emerald eyes. Caledonia would not find fault in her fashion choices. As always, she wore a circular pendant, this one encrusted with jet black stones. It matched the black beaded band around her forehead and the black sash cinched at her waist.

Archie pulled the car over to the side of the street. Rex recognised his grandmother's rented town house.

"Out you go, guv," Archie said with a smile. "Basil and the others are right behind."

Sure enough, Clark, Harris, and Inga were climbing out of their car. They'd clued Clark in on Inga and Harris's relationship early in the trip. He'd accepted the news of an entanglement between Dora's companion and her butler with aplomb. After three months spent travelling together, he considered them both as friends.

And so, the unlikely crew — two lords, a socialite, a companion, and a butler — entered the home of the Dowager Duchess of Rockingham for an intimate, late dinner.

Sheffield led them to the drawing room. Rex caught himself fidgeting with his button again. At the rate he was going, he'd have to hand it over to his grandmother's lady's maid for repair while they ate.

Inside, his grandmother rose from her chair and hurried over to welcome them with open arms. She embraced Dora and Inga and allowed both Harris and Clark to kiss her hand.

What she did not do was to introduce Caledonia. Mainly, because the young woman wasn't present.

Edith caught Rex glancing at the door. "Caledonia is running late. She'll join us directly in the dining room."

For the first time in his life, Rex felt both relieved and stressed at the same time. Like any man waiting to learn his fate, he wanted it over as much as he hoped to delay.

He drank his pre-dinner cocktail and let the others carry the conversation. Now and then, Dora would brush her fingers over his leg or arm, silently reminding him of her presence.

Finally, the butler called them to dinner. His grandmother sat at the head of the table with Rex on her right and Clark on her left. She instructed them to leave the seat next to Rex for Caledonia, and for Inga to sit beside her. Dora took the chair next to Clark and Harris filled in on her left.

Heels clicked in the corridor, echoing on the marble floor. A young woman entered the dining room. Pale blonde hair framed a heart-shaped face. She froze in the doorway, lingering at the threshold while viewing the table full of adults.

"Caledonia, there you are. Come in and sit next to your brother. I'll make the introductions."

"Yes, Grandmama," she murmured in a barely audible voice. She nodded at the footman who pulled out her chair. "Apologies for my tardiness."

Rex studied her profile while his grandmother rattled off everyone's name. Caledonia had inherited his grandmother's ability to hide her thoughts behind a stiff upper lip. Her wide eyes took in everything, while her expression revealed nothing.

At last, she turned to face him, drowning him in her fathomless gaze. Rex struggled to identify her emotion. Was she pleased to be reunited? Did she think him a bore?

Her first words failed to answer his question. She said, simply, "Hello, brother."

She sounded so like his grandmother. Prim, proper, reserved. But there was no disdain. At least she didn't hate him.

"Hello, Callie," he replied, using her childhood name.

Her eyes flashed with a hint of anger. "Caledonia, please. I outgrew that nickname several years ago."

Rex flinched. Two words in and he was already on the wrong foot. "Of course, of course. You're practically grown now. Nearly eighteen?"

"My birthday was last month," she muttered.

"And we celebrated it with a private dinner on board the ship," Rex's grandmother added, giving him an escape from the awkwardness. "It was the day after our departure from Southampton. We stopped in several ports along the way. I told Caledonia to consider the trip to be my birthday treat."

"How lovely for you both," Dora said, gracing Caledonia with a smile.

Caledonia gave a stiff nod in reply. Clark leapt in with an anecdote from their own travels. The conversation took on a life of its own.

Over the four-course meal, Rex did his best to surreptitiously study his sister. She loosened up with him, giving him an encouraging smile when he spoke.

Mostly, she kept quiet. It wasn't until Inga asked her about her music that Caledonia came alive.

"I came to study under Maestro Mantovani. He has instructed some of the finest piano virtuosos in the world. I'm incredibly fortunate he agreed to take me on."

"You must be very talented," Dora said, giving Caledonia a bright smile. Caledonia flushed under the praise, but didn't otherwise reply.

"Will you play something for us later?" Inga asked.

"Yes, although I should warn you, my skills may disappoint you."

Inga's brow creased. "I very much doubt that." She glanced at Edith, searching for an explanation.

"Caledonia is more than proficient, despite what she says. However, her true talent is as a musicologist. She is here to study the language of the composers rather than to master the ivory keys."

"That's incredible," Rex gasped. Caledonia flushed again.

She went on to explain her fascination with how the lives and societies around Mozart, Beethoven, and Bach had influenced their musical styles. She'd come to Rome to learn more about Verdi.

Rex paid his sister even more attention, studying her overtly now. That was when he noticed the subtle changes in her demeanour, depending upon whom she addressed.

With Inga, she was unflinchingly polite. Harris got her to unbend a couple of times. When she addressed Dora or Clark, her voice turned cold. Abrupt even.

Twice she dragged her gaze toward Rex. In both instances, because Dora and Clark shared a laugh.

There was no mistaking her emotion. Her pained glance was heavy with pity.

Rex couldn't make heads or tails of that. Surely his grandmother had alluded to his relationship with Dora, even if only in the most oblique of terms. Yes, Clark and Dora were on friendly terms. That didn't make Clark a threat to him.

His concern rose, though he did his best to tamp it down.

Caledonia didn't know. She was misinterpreting the situation. He'd set her straight.

The footmen cleared the dessert plates and his grandmother suggested they enjoy a digestive in the comfort of the drawing room. "Rex and Caledonia, do you two want to precede us into the music room? That will give you a chance to speak privately about the other matter."

"Quite sensible," Rex said. It would also give him a chance to rectify Caledonia's opinion of Dora.

The music room was on the first floor. The distance from the drawing room ensured they'd have privacy. The room featured a grand piano as the centrepiece. Chairs and a pair of sofas provided seating for the listeners. Rex eyed a pair of wooden chairs with the intent of claiming them, but Caledonia had other ideas.

She closed the door behind them and then turned to face him. "Rex, how could you?"

Rex mis-stepped and bumped against a side table. "Huh?"

"I know you'll think me too young to understand, but anyone with eyes can see she's betraying you. How could you bring her into Grandmama's home?"

"Theodora isn't betraying me! What would give you that idea?"

"These," Caledonia spat. She hurried over to the piano bench and lifted the lid of the seat. From inside the bench, she pulled a stack of newspaper cuttings. "Ever since you left England, she's been photographed with someone else as often as yourself. And this one!"

Caledonia unfolded the top page and passed it to him. The photo was from the event in Sirmione. Dora stood sandwiched between Clark and D'Annunzio, smiling slyly at the camera. The photo description hinted that there might be something more to her friendships with the men. "She is shameless!"

Dora was shameless, but not in the way Caledonia meant.

Caledonia carried on, giving him no time to reply. She pointed at a smaller photo lower down the page. "And here you are with another woman! Who is she?"

"Silvia something? I haven't the faintest," he said. When Caledonia's brows shot up, he hurried to add, "She doesn't matter. I'm committed to Theodora."

Caledonia uttered a dark laugh, one far too mature for her age. "But she's using you, Rex! Don't tell me I'm too young to know. The musical world is filled with stories of harlots and fortune-hunters. She fits the mould to a tee."

Caledonia's refusal to say Dora's name got to him the most.

He squared his shoulders and met her gaze head on. "Her name is Theodora, and I'd take care how you speak of her."

"Why?" Callie tossed her pale blonde hair over her shoulder. "She'll move on to some other bloke soon enough."

Rex's throat burned with fury. "Theodora will never leave me."

Caledonia sniffed in disbelief.

Rex clenched his fists. His little sister, now a grown woman, looked at him with such disdain. He lost all control over himself. His planned conversation flew out the window.

"Dora is my wife!"

Caledonia gasped and swayed on her feet. Rex was shocked to find he was also standing. His mouth opened, but no words came out.

"You married her?" Caledonia's eyes flicked left and right as she weighed her next move. Her eyes narrowed until her knife-sharp glare pinned him in place. "I'm telling Grandmama."

"Grandmama knows." Rex sighed heavily. "She gave us her blessing."

"No." Caledonia shook her head furiously. "You're lying to keep me quiet."

Rex crossed the room and grasped his sister's hands. He opened his eyes wide and met her head on. "I promise, I speak the truth. Ask Grandmama anything you want, but not until you are alone. This secret is worth more than Dora's life. Nothing is as it seems, Callie. There is only so much I can tell."

Caledonia searched his face. "Dora? Is that what you call her?"

Rex nodded.

"Is Theodora even her name?"

Rex sucked in a breath and then sealed his lips shut. She was far too adept at piecing together the puzzle. If the clips from the society pages were any sign, she'd been following their movements for months.

He and Dora had no one to blame but themselves. They'd played the role of unfettered lovers too well. The vultures at the gossip rags loved nothing more than to speculate over the longevity of their relationship. Was it any wonder Caledonia thought he'd made a colossal mistake?

Rex guided her to the pair of chairs and encouraged her to sit. He needed to change the conversation topic before the others arrived.

"Tell me about the woman. The murder victim."

Caledonia swallowed, and then nodded in understanding. She took a breath to steady her nerves. "I only have suspicions. Nothing concrete."

"Any lead is useful, even if it later turns out to be wrong. We don't know where to start."

"I saw her twice, before she died... was killed," she corrected herself. "Both times in passing. It wasn't until I saw her photograph in the paper that I made the connection."

"Go on..."

"She came here, to the house, to tune the piano, last week. I heard someone playing and stuck my head in to see who it was. She leapt to her feet, apologising in broken English for getting carried away. I left her to gather her things.

That aligned with what Rex knew so far. "What about the first time?"

"It was in England. Maybe six months ago. I was at a workshop. She was there as well. I heard her speak with someone. She spoke English with no accent. No foreigner is that good."

Dora was. Rex pushed Caledonia on the point. "How much did you hear her say? Couldn't you have been mistaken?"

"Rex, they called her Mary. Not Maria, or whatever name she was using here. I'd bet all my pin money that she is as English as we are."

Chapter 6
On British Ground

L ater that night, in the privacy of their room, Rex recounted his conversation with his sister. Dora's heart went out to him. She understood better than anyone how easily such conversations could go astray. The best made intentions flew out the window when it came to family.

Truthfully, she'd known things had gone awry the moment she entered the music room. All night, Caledonia had been cool to her. Then the ice melted, to be replaced by a searching gaze. Caledonia studied her as though she was a riddle to solve.

Rex must have told her of their relationship. It was the only logical explanation. If anything, Caledonia's reaction to the news fascinated Dora.

Although she was quiet, it would be a gross mistake to underestimate her.

That didn't stop Rex from self-flagellating over his mishandling of the situation. Dora tried several times to interrupt his endless rounds of apology. He waved off her attempts. At last, she'd opted to wait until he ran out of steam.

It seemed that time was now. Rex's voice trailed off, and he hung his head. His blue mood stood in juxtaposition to the warm tones decorating their bedroom suite. Unlike in the typical upper class English home, here the top floor boasted the nicest accommodation and best views.

The night was warm enough that the balcony doors remained open. Dora took Rex by the hand and guided him outside. She pointed at the moonlit cupola off in the distance.

"Do you see that? It is Saint Peter's Basilica. For all who enter its doors, it is a place of forgiveness. Imagine yourself there and grant yourself the same mercy, darling. So your talk didn't go as planned! It ended on a high point. She trusted you with her information because you trusted her with our news. From where I stand, that is an excellent starting point for an open relationship."

Rex turned to Dora, hope lighting his blue eyes. "Do you truly think that? You aren't just saying it to make me feel better?"

"I do. I promise. Give her time. She'll succumb to my charms, eventually. Everyone always does." She fluffed her hair to emphasise her confidence, coaxing a laugh from her husband.

Rex pulled her close and stole her breath with a searing kiss. When she broke free, she led him back into the bedroom.

The next morning, both in decidedly better humour, they joined the others at the breakfast table. Clark was making a valiant effort to try one of each of the pastries Nonna Matilda had prepared. He nudged the platter toward Rex and begged him to lend a hand.

Over steaming cappuccinos, they agreed on a plan for the day.

"Our first stop must be the embassy. Sir Francis promised to arrange credentials for us. Clark, come as well. As a member of the House of Lords, you are the most senior official in the country after the ambassador. Should we need it, your name and title will help open doors."

Clark felt thrilled to be of service. "So long as I'm not required to sit through endless debates over inconsequential political matters, I'm glad to lend a hand."

"Hold tight to that thought. By the time we get to the bottom of this mess, we'll likely all be ready to embrace a little boredom."

"Shall I ring for the car?" Rex asked while dusting pastry crumbs from his lapel.

"Yes, but have them pick us up from the embassy in time for lunch." Dora eyed the plate of crumbs. "We're going to walk there."

"Walk?" Clark spluttered, looking positively aghast. "In these shoes? My valet will have my head."

Dora wagged a finger at him. "How will your valet react when he has to let out all your waistbands? Skiing, hiking and sightseeing have saved you thus far. If we mean to keep in shape here, then we should walk when we can. Besides, it is the best way to explore all of Rome's delights."

Clark gave in with good grace, but Dora spotted him helping himself to a last almond croissant. After changing into comfortable shoes and grabbing their things, the trio set off.

It was a gorgeous spring day. In any other place, one would hear the birds chirping and smell the blooming flowers. But in the centre of Rome, only the pigeons fought for space on the roofs and lamp posts. Instead of gardens, there were fountains and window boxes.

Dora didn't mind. Rome was on her shortlist of favourite places to visit. She'd never been able to pick just one. She counted herself fortunate to have found a life where she'd never have to do so.

However, it wasn't her love of Rome that slowed her steps. This case was as complex as the city itself. The ambassador had a history here. How many people had he angered or snubbed over the years? Dora had much to learn before she'd find the solution.

As they walked, she pointed out the landmarks. One street held a Roman temple. The piazzas played host to Renaissance sculptures and elaborately carved fountains. Interwoven between it all, new construction helped the city evolve. One was always uncertain of what awaited around the next corner.

Rex and Clark were happy to let her play tour guide.

"You've read far more than I have," Clark confessed.

"I often daydreamed during my Latin lessons," Rex added.

Dora glanced over her shoulder at him. "I thought that was your German lessons where you failed to pay attention."

"There, too, " Rex said in chagrin. "I take full responsibility for my shortcomings in German. But for Latin, that was the fault of my teacher."

"How so?" Dora asked.

"He assigned me pages upon pages of stories about emperors conquering the world. Two pages into my lesson and I was busy imagining the battle scenes. Before I knew it, my notebook was half-full of doodles."

"I remember that!" Clark said. "You drew the best gladiators and centurions of anyone in our year."

"I'll keep that in mind should our situation call for illustrations. In the meantime, pay attention."

"Yes, Mistress Laurent," both men uttered in unison.

Dora rolled her eyes and kept walking. This was her fault, really. She'd brought them into her life, knowing full well they were incorrigible.

The sight of the British flag waving in the breeze recalled her to the present. She wiped all traces of humour from her mind as they approached the entrance to the British embassy. She remembered every hall and doorway like the lines on the back of her hand. She had to be extra careful not to reveal that fact.

During her prior investigation, she'd donned a black wig and used bronzing powder to darken her skin. Night after night, she'd pushed a mop along the corridors as part of the cleaning crew. No one paid the slightest attention when she entered offices.

Had she wanted, she could have walked out with the state secrets. Instead, her task was to plug the gap. After the death of the ambassador's private secretary, Lord Audley had sent a team to implement a new security regime.

Was that the root cause of their current problem? Was someone trying to rid themselves of Sir Francis, hoping to have someone more amenable put in charge?

If so, they were staring down the barrel of an international scandal.

Dora shuddered at the thought.

"Everything all right, darling?" Rex asked.

"Don't mind me. I'm being silly," she answered. "I've not been inside a British embassy in a while. Here's hoping they don't lock me inside and throw away the key."

"With us here to rally to your defence?" Clark shook his head. "We'll have a cup of proper tea and pretend we're on British soil for an hour."

Dora allowed Clark to offer his arm. He escorted her through the front door and up to a desk manned by a guard. Rex followed behind.

"Hello, old chap. I'm Lord Clark Kenworthy, representing the House of Lords. I believe Sir Francis sent word that we were to be expected."

The guard blinked a few times, clearly at a loss. He remembered himself and flipped through a pile of papers, searching for Clark's name. When he came up short, he asked them to take a seat.

The lack of immediate recognition appalled Clark. Dora soothed him by reminding him he skipped more sessions in the house than he attended.

"Yes, but does the man not read the papers? I'm featured almost as often as the Prime Minister."

Rex and Dora both had to bite their lips to keep from laughing out loud.

The three paid little attention to the other people waiting. Dora caught an older man eyeing them over the top of his paper. She winked at him and he ducked out of sight.

A man emerged from the door on the other side of the guard's desk. After a brief exchange, the uniformed guard pointed him their way.

"Lord Clark, my deepest apologies," the man said while wringing his hands. "Due to a last minute change in the schedule, we are at sixes and sevens today."

Clark was far too easygoing to hold a grudge. He assured the man that no offence had been taken.

"If you'll follow me, I'll show you to a private space where you can wait."

Dora studied the embassy man. She estimated him to be in his early thirties. His brown hair was on the longer side and slicked back with hair oil. It almost hid the burn scars rising along his neck. Dora suspected his moustache and beard hid more scars. He was a war veteran, then. One of the many soldiers for whom the government found work after the war ended.

The man shifted between his normal pace — a fast gait that ate up the floor — and a slower one when he remembered they were following. Not a senior staff member, she decided. How had he drawn the short straw and ended up responsible for them?

He showed them to a well appointed sitting room and invited them to make themselves comfortable. He scurried off and returned soon after with a tea tray.

"Again, I offer my apologies. With Sir Francis fearing to leave his home, he called all the section heads to work from there."

"It's no problem at all, Mr—"

"Shaw. Brandon Shaw. My goodness, I didn't even introduce myself!" The man cringed at his mistake. "I'm a clerk here at the embassy, in Sir Francis's office."

"It's a pleasure to meet you, Mr Shaw. I assume you know why we are here," Clark said.

"Oh yes. The paperwork!" Mr Shaw glanced down at his empty hands and he blanched. "It's on my desk."

When he leapt to his feet, Dora could take it no more. She held up a hand to forestall him.

"Please, sit," she said in her French accent. "We are in no rush, and you seem run off your feet. Let's enjoy a cup of your English tea and chat while you catch your breath."

Mr Shaw half-turned toward his chair, but stopped before he sat. Knowing Sir Francis as she did, Dora was confident the ambassador had never taken tea with his underlings. He glanced at Clark and Rex to make sure they approved of him following Dora's suggestion.

Rex encouraged him to sit and even went so far as to pour the man a cup of tea.

Now that Dora had taken control of the situation, she had no intention of relinquishing it. She asked Mr Shaw about his role and how long he'd been stationed in Rome.

"Rome was my first posting after the war. I started as a

junior clerk in the typing pool and have gradually worked my way up."

Dora didn't remember him from before, but that wasn't a surprise. She'd focused her attention on those with ready access to secret information. A typist wouldn't have made the cut.

Now, however, he worked directly for the ambassador.

"Did Sir Francis explain why we are here?" Dora asked. When Brandon shook his head, she explained, "We've promised to help Sir Francis sort out this murder accusation. Given you work closely with him, you must have an opinion on the matter."

Brandon blanched. "I'm nowhere near an equal to Sir Francis. His private secretary would be a much better person to ask. All I do is type notes and see that documents are delivered to the right individuals."

Rex picked up the thread. "I'm sure you know more than you think. Surely, you must overhear the ambassador's discussions. Or what of the meeting notes? Can you recollect any mentions of people who disagreed with the ambassador?"

Brandon shook his head. "Oh no, my lord. It isn't my place to make a judgement on such matters."

Dora gritted her teeth. The man was determined to avoid stating an opinion. She studied his body language, searching for any hint of whether he'd respond better to an overture of friendship or an order to comply.

Clark took the decision out of her hands. "We aren't asking you to determine who is right or wrong on such occasions, Mr Shaw. But it would be helpful if you could offer any indications of who might hold a grudge against Sir Francis."

Dora noticed a fine sheen of sweat dotting Brandon's forehead. Why was the man so nervous? Was he terrified of someone within the embassy or of them?

Clark was growing annoyed by Mr Shaw's constant dodging of the questions. He set his teacup down, squared his shoulders, and looked the man in the face. "Mr Shaw, I need you to understand the situation. Sir Francis stands accused of murder. While diplomatic immunity will save his head, it won't rescue his reputation. We are not angling for gossip. We're in search of other suspects."

Mr Shaw's cheeks paled even more. "I know nothing. I can't help. You must speak with the ambassador."

Clark refused to back down. "We've heard from him. Now, I want your thoughts. Do you think Sir Francis is guilty of the crime?"

Brandon choked. "What? No! Of course not! Everyone here holds him in the highest regard. I should get your authorisation so that you can better investigate the matter." He dashed from the room like the hounds of hell were nipping at his heels.

Dora, Rex, and Clark exchanged glances. None had an explanation for his behaviour. They all agreed it was strange.

He returned before they had a chance to discuss further. He passed an envelope to Clark. "The requisite documents are inside, along with the name and contact information for the lead investigator at the Carabinieri. He is expecting you to visit this afternoon."

Clark thanked him for his help and tucked the envelope in his inside coat pocket. "Should anything else come to mind, or any relevant information come to light, please send word."

"Of course, my lord. Where are you staying?"

Dora cut in before Clark could reply. "You can reach us at the residence of Rex's grandmother. The Dowager Duchess of Rockingham," she added.

Brandon Shaw nodded and didn't ask for the address. As Dora expected, he knew who the dowager was. She cast a long shadow, and that was what Dora was counting upon.

Chapter 7
Society Takes Note

"Why did you give him Grandmama's address?" Rex asked once they were back outside.

Dora spotted the car parked further down the road and began walking toward it. "The man was nervous, but why? Does Sir Francis terrify him? Someone else in the embassy? I thought it wise to offer him a safe port in the oncoming storm."

Rex whistled. "Mighty clever of you, my dear. In any battle, I'd place my money on grandmama."

"Me, too," Clark agreed. "Which is why I'll leave it to you to explain to her about her new houseguests."

Rex laughed as expected, but he wasn't in the least concerned. His grandmother loved being part of their adventures.

At home, they found Nonna Matilda waiting for them. She showed them into the dining room and explained the seating arrangements. "Teodora, you and Signor Rex sit here." She indicated the other side of the table. "Inga and Harris, you may sit across from them."

"And me?" Clark asked, growing concerned.

Nonna Matilda beamed at him as she took him by the arm.

"You are the guest of honour today, Signor Clark. For you, I have prepared extra dishes."

She wasn't lying. For every dish Rex sampled, Clark tried two. By the time the meal was over, Clark's eyelids had a definite droop.

Clark groaned, belched softly, and then blushed in embarrassment. "Goodness me, I'm so stuffed I can hardly move."

"Move, you must," Rex chided his friend. "We're due to meet with the Carabinieri soon."

Clark's eyes widened, and he stared at Rex in horror. "I forgot! How did I forget?" he surveyed his place setting until his gaze landed on his wineglass. "Why'd you let me indulge in that third glass of wine? I can hardly show up in a police station smelling of alcohol."

Dora came to his rescue. "Rex and I can go. It's likely to be dreadfully boring, anyway."

Rex felt Dora tap him on his leg under the table. He chimed in. "Theodora is right. I can't imagine the local police are thrilled to have us checking their work. They'll likely make us cool our heels for ages. No need for all three of us to suffer. We'll bring everything back here and we can review it together."

"Are you sure?" Clark glanced at the faces around the table. "I feel terrible. I promised to help you with this."

Dora tilted her head to the side and feigned an expression of deep concentration. "There is one thing you could do..."

"Anything!"

Dora grinned at Clark and then turned to Harris. "Did you pick up copies of the Sunday papers?"

"I did, indeed. The English bookshop you recommended had both the Sunday Pictorial and the Sunday Express. Hold on, I'll go fetch them."

While Harris hurried to the next room to retrieve the

papers, Rex threw up his hands in disgust. "Not those vapid society columns again! I asked you two to swear off reading that drivel. The columnists make a mockery of everyone in our set, present company included! If you believe them, our lives are spent entirely at endless parties, drinking, doing drugs, partner-swapping, and every other sort of debauchery under the sun they imagine. It's an affront, I tell you!"

Harris returned in time to catch the tail end of Rex's rant. He wagged his finger. "It's what sells, Rex. You'll find Casper Eadmund's Sunday column particularly interesting. You and Dora warranted a mention."

"What?" Rex rose from his chair and grabbed the paper from Harris's outstretched hand. He didn't have to search for the article as Harris had folded the paper so it would be on top.

As usual, Eadmund utilised thinly veiled nicknames to describe his prey. Rex and Dora had featured often enough to have earned a proper moniker.

It took Rex no time to find their mention. "Here we are. *Rumour has it Lord Caesar and his paramour Goldy are on their way to Rome. Can they help Drake with his tight squeeze? Stay tuned!* Drake must be Sir Francis, correct?"

Dora jerked sideways as though she'd been struck. "What's the date on that paper?"

"This Sunday," Harris answered. "The day before you arrived."

Rex caught up with Dora's whip smart mind. "How did Eadmund know we were coming? To make the Sunday publication date, he'd have had to uncover that tidbit before we knew ourselves."

"Harris and I debated the matter while you all were at the embassy. Everyone knows that Casper Eadmund is a pseudonym. Thus far, no one has managed to uncover the writer's identity. But perhaps with Clark's assistance, we might finally do the impossible."

"My assistance?" Clark paled. "It isn't me, if that's what you're insinuating!"

Inga scoffed at the mere idea. "Of course you aren't the writer. But you mentioned seeing a bunch of journalists yesterday. Sir Francis must have spoken to one of them, or somehow let slip his plan to reach out for help. It is a simple enough matter to uncover when they arrived and who had the chance to speak with the ambassador."

Clark rubbed his stomach, still looking slightly green at the gills. "I'll give it a go, but I must admit, I have no idea how this helps us with the investigation."

"Consider it honing your sleuthing skills. Our murderer is hiding in plain sight. So, too, is the person behind the ridiculous pen name."

Harris leaned forward. "And if that isn't enough to keep you occupied, I've got one other matter that could benefit from your expertise. While I was out, I purchased two new pairs of shoes and I don't know which pair to keep."

"That's simple — keep both!" Clark said before throwing back his head in a boisterous laugh.

Inga rapped on the table and glared at both Clark and Harris in turn. "None of that! Your travel trunk is full to bursting as it is. If something new is to come in, something else must go out."

Clark never could resist a fashion challenge. He ceded the envelope from the embassy to Rex and followed Harris out of the room.

As soon as they were out of earshot, Dora took the envelope from Rex and pulled out the paper. She skimmed it before handing it back.

"As expected, it only provides authorisation for you and

Clark. It's a good thing I already prepared a back-up plan. But to pull it off, I needed Clark to be busy elsewhere."

Rex's focus slipped from his place setting to Clark's. Surely Dora had not...

"You tampered with his food!" he gasped.

Dora placed her hand on her chest. "Me? I was with you all morning."

Inga, who was still sitting with them, took pity on him. "There was no need to resort to treachery. No one eats that many rounds of pasta and meat and remains upright."

"We'd best get to work before Clark finishes his tasks." Rex turned to Dora. "How long do you need to don whatever disguise you have in mind?"

"Not long at all. Cynthia should have everything I need in the guest house. Why don't you have a coffee and then meet me at the car?"

Rex took his time sipping his espresso, and even permitted himself two of Mathilda's crunchy biscuits. When he judged that enough time had passed, he went outside.

There was no sign of Dora's reddish blonde bob, nor of her usual finery. Instead, a demure woman in a frumpy dress, glasses, and a curly brown wig waited in the back seat.

"Who are you today?" he asked after he slid inside.

"Sir! Do you not recognise your translator?"

"Of course, silly me," he answered, playing along. He was impressed by her London accent tinged with a hint of the Italian rolling R. "But if you'd be so kind as to remind me of your name."

"Signora Lorenzo."

Rex chuckled. Leave it to Dora to find endless variations of her pseudonym.

* * *

As Archie and Basil had taken the afternoon off for a visit to the Roman Forum, one of Nonna Matilda's servants drove the car. The wizened Italian man whizzed in and out of traffic, paying little heed to horns or traffic signs. Somehow, they arrived at the large office building in one piece.

A pair of Ionic columns flanked the front entrance. The steady flow of men in crisp navy uniforms, each bearing the insignia of the military's police force, rendered the sign next to the front door unnecessary.

"I expected something less grand for a police station," Rex said, gazing at the impressive building.

"The Italians do nothing by half measure. For a case as high-profile as this one, it's no surprise our contact works at the organisation's headquarters."

Dora told Rex to take the lead. She followed behind as befitted her status as his assistant. When they arrived at the front desk, he stepped aside and motioned for her to speak on his behalf.

"Buongiorno, Signore Bankes-Fernby é qui per una reunione," she said in flawless Italian.

Rex meandered around the building lobby while Dora explained who they were and why they were there.

In most respects, it was not that different from the government offices back home. In places of pride hung photographs of King Vittorio Emanuele, Prime Minister Mussolini, and the current leader of the Carabinieri.

But a closer inspection showed that the carpet bore signs of wear, and the wooden chairs were scratched. Underneath the proud face it showed the world, post-war Italy bore signs of underinvestment.

Rex had studied this as part of their background briefing for the mission. Although Italy had emerged as a victor of the Great War, they ended up with a much smaller portion of the spoils.

The Italians felt disrespected by England and the United States.

Mussolini was able to capitalise on the nationalistic spirit to catapult himself into power. They were a proud nation and were certain they deserved better. Mussolini promised he would deliver a much brighter future, no matter the cost.

Was punishing the British ambassador part of Mussolini's plan? Sir Francis was convinced it was not. Rex wished he were as sure.

"Lord Reginald," Dora called in her Italian translator voice. "They are ready for us."

Rex caught her eye and raised a brow. Already? Like she'd told Clark, he also expected to be kept waiting. Instead, the officer manning the desk showed them through a pair of carved wooden doors and into a busy office.

Men bustled around the room while still more sat behind desks. The only other woman in sight was emptying a rubbish bin. This was a man's world, not that an English police department would be any different.

The officer rapped on a closed door. A voice inside called for them to enter.

"Signor Bankes-Fernsby, il rappresentante dell'ambasciata Inglese, é qui." The officer stepped back to allow Rex and Dora inside.

The private office took up one corner of the building. In the far corner sat a heavy desk buried under piles of papers. Closer to the door was a small seating area. Thin drapes covered the floor-to-ceiling windows, blocking the direct sunlight while still allowing a pleasant glow to illuminate the space. A distinguished man in his sixties rose from behind the desk and came to greet Rex. He drew up short when he saw Dora follow behind.

"Signora Lorenzo is my translator," Rex explained. He steeled his gaze to prevent any argument.

"I am Lucio Grandi, Generale Commandante of the Carabinieri. I understand you are here to learn more about the pending charges against your ambassador."

"I am. This is a serious matter. It is best for everyone that no mistakes are made."

Rex half expected the man to argue, or become defensive, but his welcoming demeanour did not change.

"On this, we can agree. It is what you English call an open and shut case. However, due to the political nature of the suspect, the Prime Minister asked me to delay making a formal accusation. So, let us have a seat. I have a copy of the investigation file for you."

Generale Grandi took a wingback chair, leaving the sofa for Dora and Rex.

Dora took care to leave the appropriate amount of space between them. Rex bit back a smile when she adjusted her glasses and pursed her lips, showing an incredible amount of concentration.

Grandi handed Rex a file. Rex flipped it open. Unsurprisingly, it was written in Italian. He passed it to Dora. "My Italian is passable, but not robust enough to handle the police vocabulary. I would very much appreciate hearing an overview."

Grandi crossed his hands over his stomach and sank into the chair, seemingly relaxed despite the situation.

Rex prepared himself not to react, no matter what the man told him.

"In the early hours of fifteen May, your ambassador strangled a woman outside the gates of his home. He left her there, in the shadow of a large tree, and went back inside. A passerby discovered her body at daybreak."

"Begging your pardon, Generale Grandi, but you seem awfully confident of the timing and sequence of events."

The generale's mouth upticked on one side. He was not put out by the interruption. "The victim had the ambassador's card in her pocket and held his lapel pin in her fist. We believe she pulled it from his coat during the struggle. Those facts led us to consider the ambassador a suspect. We didn't narrow in on him exclusively until a witness stepped forward. Her testimony confirmed his identity. We informed the Prime Minister, he asked us to hold off on making any statements until your embassy had a chance to review our findings. Now, you are here."

A witness? That information was certainly unexpected and cast the ambassador's claims in a new light. Rex didn't need to glance at Dora to know what question she'd want him to ask. "Might we be able to speak with this witness?"

"I have put her name and address in the file and told her to expect a visit. But please, go easy on her. She is cieca."

Czech? Why should her nationality make any difference? Rex kept that question to himself. Likely, Dora would know. "What of the victim?"

"We know her only as Maria Cacciatore. We searched her rented room, but the only identifying papers we found were false. Her employer could tell us little else about her. You are welcome to speak to him. I've included his details in the folder."

Rex waited to see if the man would add anything else, but he rose from his chair, signalling he was done. Rex and Dora followed suit.

Rex replayed the generale's words on his way back through the building. A lapel pin and a card were hardly proof positive of the ambassador's presence on the scene. They needed to focus their attention on the testimony of the foreign witness.

But how to approach her? Generale Grandi's advice had been clear, even if it made little sense.

When they got in the car, Rex finally got the chance to ask. " Why did the generale warn us to go easy on the Czech woman?"

"Not Czech," Dora said. "He said *cieca*, Rex. Their so-called witness is blind."

Chapter 8
The Lady of the House

I n any other circumstances, Dora would have chuckled over
Rex's translation mistake. This situation, however, left them
with nothing about which to laugh. When they got home, Dora
hurried to change out of her disguise. Dressed again as herself,
she and Rex shared the news with Clark.

Clark goggled at Dora and Rex. "Are you playing some kind
of joke on me? A blind witness? Surely you misunderstood!"

Dora's serious expression didn't shift. "You've watched me
converse with Italians over the past few weeks. Do you
honestly believe I'd make a mistake of this magnitude?" She
opened the folder and flipped to the correct page. "Check for
yourself."

Clark took the folder and scrunched his brow while he
skimmed over the words. His reaction did not surprise Dora.
Rex had spent the drive home in stunned silence.

Clark closed the folder and dropped it onto the coffee table.
It landed with a splat. "I have never heard anything so ridiculous
in my life! The eyewitness can't see! Do they think we're fools?"

Rex glanced at Dora, his eyebrow raised to echo Clark's
question. "I agree that the evidence is flimsy. From how

everyone spoke, I assumed the Carabinieri had a smoking gun, or a bloodied shirt."

"The murderer strangled the woman," Dora pointed out. She steepled her fingers like Lord Audley often did and tried to think like him. What could cause the spymaster to utilise such a tactic?

She began by assuming the case was solid and the Carabinieri had a witness. Who could have been watching the ambassador? Someone like her, that's who. Audley would never let any of his agents take the witness box. He'd search high and low until he identified an alternative.

A passerby had discovered the victim's body on the pavement. The Carabinieri couldn't hush up the case. The people of Rome would expect answers, and rightly so. It made sense. Accepting the testimony of a blind woman made their lives easy. They got credit for identifying the murderer. More importantly, this solution kept the British from finding out they were being spied upon.

Yet, there remained a flaw in that logic. If all that were true, why would Mussolini and Vittorio Emanuele give Sir Francis time to clear his name?

Dora set that line of thought aside and moved on to the second possibility. The flimsy evidence was meant to send a message. Sir Francis was no longer welcome in Italy.

She shared her thoughts with the men.

Clark ran a hand through his hair. "What if we're making too much of this witness? Is it at all possible that the Carabinieri are willing to accept the testimony of a blind woman?" When Dora and Rex failed to answer, he huffed in frustration. "We need to talk to Sir Francis again. I haven't seen him yet. Perhaps I will spot some tell that will give us a fresh clue."

Dora did not have a better suggestion. "If we go now, we should catch him before dinner."

The trio rode across town, all staring out the windows without noticing their surroundings. Far weightier matters kept them occupied. Outside the motorcar, traffic dogged the streets. The extra time heightened everyone's frustration.

They wanted answers that made sense, and were determined not to leave until they had them.

Clark charged ahead after the car stopped in front of the ambassador's home. Dora and Rex caught up in time to hear him give their names to the butler.

"I'm sorry, my lord, but Sir Francis isn't in right now."

"Isn't in? Where would he go?" Clark asked. "He's too terrified to leave the house grounds.'"

The butler was unmoved. "I'm not at liberty to say. Shall I pass on a message?"

Clark widened his stance. "I refuse to accept this. Don't you know who we are and why we're here? Sir Francis must be inside. I insist you take us to him."

The butler flushed with the indignation gained by years in service. "I'll do no such thing! As I stated, he isn't available."

"Away or unavailable? Which is it, man?" Clark growled. He shifted his stance until his right foot crossed the threshold. He wasn't going anywhere except inside.

"Jenkins, what's the matter?" a feminine voice asked from inside the house.

The butler shifted his stance, allowing Dora a view of the grand staircase. A woman stood halfway down, with her eyes wide with concern. Dora recognised her immediately, but struggled to recall her name.

Clark, however, was quicker off the mark. "Prudence! What are you doing here?"

The butler intervened before she replied. "These people wish to speak with the ambassador. I've explained he is unavailable, but they refuse to go."

Prudence paused on the staircase and leaned sideways, looking past the butler and Clark. If she was surprised to find Dora and Rex, her expression gave no sign of it. "It's quite alright, Jenkins. I doubt Lord Clark, Lord Rex, or Miss Laurent harbour any ill intentions toward Sir Francis. I can play host in his absence."

The butler sniffed, but otherwise held his tongue. He moved aside, letting the group enter, and took the men's hats. "The marigold room is free, Miss Prudence. Shall I show them there?"

"There's no need. If you'd be so kind as to arrange for some tea and biscuits, that will be sufficient." She waited until he nodded his confirmation before leading the way to an ostentatious drawing room decorated in vibrant yellow tones. She chose an intimate seating area near the windows and invited them to sit. Dora and Rex settled upon a settee, leaving the two chairs for Prudence and Clark.

The room lived up to its name. The settee and chairs boasted white silk upholstery, providing a stark contrast to the rich yellow painted walls and gold and orange rugs. A vase of fresh marigolds sitting on a circular pedestal table in the centre of the room perfumed the air.

Of greater interest to Dora was their hostess. Her mind had finally filled in the missing blanks. She'd crossed paths with Miss Prudence Adams at many a society event, although the women had never been formally introduced. Where Dora preferred to command the centre of the room, Prudence lingered near the wall, watching instead of participating.

Only now did Dora think to ask herself why the woman had never engaged. She was more than passably attractive, with light brown hair and hazel eyes. Her eyebrows were a shade too thick, and her lips too thin, but with the right cosmetics, she'd shine. Dora knew that for certain because she employed similar tricks to elevate her appearance from ordinary woman to femme fatale.

Instead, Prudence seemed ill at ease under the spotlight. Although she played hostess, she remained silent, providing them space to offer an explanation for their unexpected visit.

The trouble was that none of them had a clue what to say. They could hardly make demands of her. They didn't even know why she was there.

Jenkins arrived bearing the requisite tea tray. He deposited it on a side table and took his leave. The tea, at least, gave a safe topic of conversation.

"I'll pour," Prudence offered. "Would everyone like a cup? Miss Laurent, how do you take yours?"

"With a splash of milk and one sugar," Dora replied. "Please, call me Theodora. Might I call you Prudence?"

Prudence agreed to the request while finishing pouring the tea. When everyone had a ceramic cup in hand, Dora slid her foot slowly over and tapped it against Rex's.

He froze for a second and then cleared his throat. "Apologies for barging in as we did. We have an urgent need to speak with Sir Francis. We weren't aware you were in residence."

Prudence brushed aside the remark. "I'm hardly interesting enough to warrant a mention in the society columns. I came down a few weeks ago, after Prince Albert's wedding. Lady Emily wanted to extend her stay in England, but dreaded the thought of leaving her husband without a proper hostess. As I'd always been keen to visit, she suggested I fill in until her return. Of course, we had no way of knowing what stress was to come. Now, I'm doubly glad I'm here."

"So, you are aware of the accusations against Sir Francis?" Clark asked.

She gave Clark a weak smile. "He's been at sixes and sevens

since he learned he is the only suspect. Getting word that you were coming provided him with so much relief. That said, I daresay the man has barely shut an eye. By this afternoon, he'd descended to such a state that I asked Jenkins to ring the doctor. He prescribed something to help Sir Francis get some rest. Upon his advice, Sir Francis turned in early."

She didn't need to fill in the gaps. Dora read between the lines. Sir Francis was in a laudanum-induced stupor and was in no state to entertain anyone. Not even them.

"But enough about things here. Is there something I can do while Sir Francis is indisposed?" Prudence's low-lashed gaze slid from Clark to Rex, waiting for one of them to answer.

"We had more questions to ask Sir Francis about the circumstances surrounding the murder. Since you're here, might we ask for your thoughts? You've been staying with Sir Francis. What do you make of the accusations against him?'"

"They are ridiculous."

Dora eyed Prudence over the rim of her teacup. "You seem confident."

Prudence shrugged. "As you said, I've had plenty of chances to interact with him over the years. Even when on holiday, the man doesn't set foot outside the house without an entourage in tow. The suggestion that he was outside the grounds, in the dead of night, with some random woman, is ludicrous. I doubt he even knows how to unlock the door!"

"Surely he isn't so incompetent..."

Prudence shook her head, cutting Dora off. "Come now, Theodora. You've met Sir Francis. Can you envision him having anything to do with a woman outside his social class? If his wife hadn't insisted I stand in for her, I wouldn't be here. Ask him and he'll tell you himself. His dearest friends are kings and queens. His drinking buddies oversee dukedoms and governing bodies. There is no way a piano tuner would cross his path."

"Do you have a piano here?" Rex asked, breaking into Prudence's monologue.

"We do, in the music room. And before you ask, yes, we had it tuned. But Sir Francis was closed up in a meeting at the time. He never saw the woman. I doubt he even knew the piano was out of tune. I requested the repair, and Jenkins oversaw her work."

Dora searched her mind for another avenue of questions but came up short.

Clark opened his mouth, choked on a word, cleared his throat and tried again. "Did you speak with the piano tuner?"

Prudence lifted her chin. "Is this your master plan, Clark? Do you intend to pin the murder on me in order to save Sir Francis? If so, you're wasting your time. What motive could I possibly have?"

Clark blanched. "It is nothing personal, Prudence. If we're to solve this mystery, we have to ask everyone the same question."

Prudence's expression softened. "You are right, of course. I wish I could help. No one here knows why this is happening. We are all as lost as Sir Francis."

Dora sensed they'd get nothing more from Prudence. Until Dora knew more about the woman, she had no idea which angle to take. A well-timed retreat was in order.

Dora set her cup and saucer on the table. "We've kept you long enough, particularly given we weren't expected." She rose from her seat and motioned for the men to follow. Before they reached the drawing-room door, Prudence spoke out.

"Should you have any other questions, please do not hesitate to get in touch. Given the situation, I'm at loose ends. I might as well help any way that I can."

Since Dora was bringing up the rear, she turned back to

reply. "That's very much appreciated. Should we require an extra pair of hands, I'll give you a ring."

A flicker of satisfaction crossed Prudence's face, but it was gone as fast as it appeared. If Dora hadn't been watching so carefully, she'd have missed it entirely.

The world might think Prudence Adams was nothing more than a wallflower. Dora had a suspicion they were very wrong.

Chapter 9
What the Blind Saw

R ex led the way out the front door and to the motorcar.
Once inside, he looked to Dora for guidance. "Where do
we go now?"

"For a walk," Dora replied, with no hesitation. After they
passed through the house gate and onto the road outside, she
instructed their driver to pull over and wait for them to
return.

Her strange instructions shook Clark out of his stupor. "A
walk? Here? My feet are still smarting from this morning."

Dora motioned for him to exit the car. When the three of
them arrived at the pavement, she provided an explanation.

"The murder took place outside the wall encircling the
grounds. Since we're here, it seems sensible to take a look." She
glanced across the street and then pointed to their left. "We'll go
this way."

The wide pavement left room enough for them to walk in a
line. Dora linked arms with the men and they set off.

"Prudence Adams in Rome," Clark muttered. "That is not a
sight I ever expected to see."

"Why not?" Dora asked, turning her head his way. "I

thought all you Brits eventually toured the major European cities."

"We do... but Prudence?" Clark leaned forward to catch Rex's eye. "You agree with me, right?"

Rex did, indeed, but Dora demanded an explanation.

"I've seen her at plenty of society events, but never at any of the clubs. Is she any relation to Lady Portia Huntley? Wasn't Portia originally an Adams before she married Lord Geoffrey?"

Rex took care not to stumble over a buckle in the pavement. "Prudence is Portia's first cousin. Clark, you should be the one to explain. You had close ties to the family."

Clark guffawed. "That's one way to put it. Portia and I were once promised to each other."

Dora pulled to a halt, dragging the men with her. "You? Engaged?" She shook her head feverishly. "No, I can't imagine it. You're putting one over."

"No, no, my dearest Theodora," Clark assured her, with a perfectly straight face. He coaxed her forward. "Rex can attest to my truthfulness. Our parents made the arrangements and assumed we'd abide by the agreement. The ending of our relationship was the only good thing to come out of the Great War."

"Who ended it?"

"We exchanged a grand total of two letters during my first year away. We simply had nothing to say to one another. Then Geoffrey took a hit in his leg and returned to England to convalesce. He ended up at Portia's grandmother's estate. Portia nursed him back to health, and he won her heart. She waited until I was home on leave to break the news in person. Honestly, we were both relieved. There were no hard feelings," he rushed to assure her.

"Very well. I accept your tale. But we've got off track. You were going to tell me about Prudence. I'd like to make use of her offer to help, but I haven't a clue what to ask. She's a veritable enigma."

"I suspect much of that is by design," Rex murmured loud enough to be heard over the passing traffic. "She hasn't had the easiest of lives."

"Oh?" Dora glanced his way and then over to Clark.

"Lord Adams is Prudence's uncle. Her father was the youngest of the four sons. Portia's father inherited the title, the spare remained home. The third son took a military commission. That left one son to dedicate to the church. Prudence's father became the vicar." Clark paused for a moment. "Prudence spent her early years in the village."

Dora asked. "How does the vicar's daughter come to be part of the London elite?"

"That's a sad tale. Her parents died in an accident when she was ten. The double loss devastated everyone, but none more than Prudence, understandably. Portia's family took her in. They made sure she lacked for nothing."

But all she'd wanted was her old life... or, at least, so Rex imagined. He hadn't known Clark then. By the time he met Portia and Prudence, they were in their teens. Prudence rarely ever joined in on the fun.

Great loss had a way of stealing the gaiety from life. Rex had seen hundreds of soldiers, friends and enemies alike, perish on the battlefield, leaving behind black scars in his memory. Sometimes the night terrors forced him to relive those days.

At least in war, one became hardened against such loss. His memories couldn't compare with losing someone from the immediate family. Like Dora's family had experienced with the death of her younger brother, William.

The same thought must have crossed Dora's mind. She pulled her hand free and dashed a tear from her face. Rex called to halt and pulled her into his arms. He held her for a moment, giving her a chance to regain control of her emotions.

Clark stared at the two of them with horror etched into his features. He cast an anguished glance at Rex and mouthed an apology.

"She lost a brother during the war," Rex whispered.

Clark nodded, needing no other explanation. Their generation was far too familiar with suffering and loss. Some mustered on, running toward the bright lights of distraction. Others, like Prudence, preferred to remain in the shadows.

Finally, Dora pulled free of his hold. He handed her his handkerchief. While she dried her face, he and Clark took in their surroundings. They'd come nearly full circle and could once again see the roofline of the ambassador's villa amidst the treetops of the grounds.

Dora called their names and pointed ahead, diverting their attention. "That tree over there. I'm certain that is our murder scene."

Rex and Clark both looked in the direction she indicated. A line of umbrella pines towered over the pavement. Their wide canopies cast shadows on the ground.

Dora hurried forward. She searched the area before coming to a stop under one of them. "This is it. It happened here."

Clark looked at the pavement. There was nothing there to mark the scene. "How can you be so sure?"

Dora motioned for him to look around. "The road narrows here and we're out of sight of the front gate. Based on where the moon would have been at the time of death, the trees would have cast this stretch in shadow."

"But isn't the same true for the trees on its right and left?" he asked.

"Yes, but if you look across the street, you'll see the building is number fifty-two. That's the address of our witness."

Clark turned his full attention on the block of flats opposite. The narrower side street had much less traffic than the wider thoroughfare further ahead. He offered Dora his arm. "Shall we go see if she is available?"

Dora linked arms with him and then encouraged Rex to take her other. In lock step, they crossed the street.

The entrance to the building was next to one of Rome's ubiquitous tiny cafes. A table with two chairs sat on the pavement in between the two doors.

Rex went straight for number fifty-two. It was locked, and a rap on it went unanswered.

"Posso aiutarvi?" a croaky voice asked.

Rex looked over to see an old woman standing in the cafe doorway. The red and green striped canopy shading the cafe front made it hard for him to get a clear view. At first glance, she reminded him of Nonna Matilda.

"Penso proprio di si," Dora replied. She stepped around the men and approached the old woman. "Are you Signora Varotti?"

Rex followed in Dora's footsteps. It was then he noticed the old woman's focus was fixed slightly to the right of them. A milky sheen clouded her eyes.

Dora had guessed correctly that the woman was their witness. She introduced herself and identified the men. Signora Varotti invited them inside the cafe as though she were the owner. The man behind the bar called her Mamma, so the guess wasn't a stretch.

"Un aperitivo, Giovanni," she ordered. When the man leapt into action she added, "He is a good boy, just like his father." She made the sign of the cross and looked to the heavens.

After that brief pause, she told them to sit.

The bar was a narrow, single room. They made use of every square inch of the room. Shelves decorated with boxes of pasta and homemade sauces lined the walls. A long counter and set of display cases took up a good third of the room. Blocks of cheeses and hocks of smoked meat filled the display.

There was an espresso machine and tiny espresso cups behind the bar. The man, Giovanni, busied himself with pouring a red-orange liquid into four red wine goblets. He added an olive and an orange wedge before loading them onto a tray.

"Campari Spritz," he explained as he handed them out. He also left two small bowls filled with an assortment of salty snacks.

Rex watched him make his way back behind the bar. How had the blind woman found her way through the tables and chairs without stumbling?

"You are here about the poveretta?" Signora Varotti asked. "I light a candle for her and say a prayer every day. May her soul find peace," she added.

Rex sipped his drink, his mouth puckering at the bitter flavour. It wasn't awful, but it was strange. Clark eyed his glass with distrust. Dora nudged Signora Varotti's glass closer to her hand.

"I am blind, but that doesn't mean I cannot see," the old woman said. She reached around her glass and plucked a snack from the bowl. "I have my mamma to thank for that. She named me Lucia."

"After the patron saint?" Dora asked.

Signora Varotti patted Dora's hand. "You are a good girl to know the origin of my name. Santa Lucia protects the blind. She sharpened my remaining senses to fill the gap of my missing sight."

She spoke in a convincing tone, but Rex couldn't entirely believe her. Her generous smile invited benevolence. Maybe it was the combination of the help of others and age that allowed her to get by.

Clark rested his hands on the table and focused on their witness. "We are here in behalf of the British government. The Carabinieri told us you saw the murder."

"That is one way to put it. In Italia, we say testimone - to give testament to the crime. For my sins, I was cursed to witness what was happening, but I could not stop it."

They settled in as she recounted the night in question.

"I do not sleep well. The air in my room was thick. I rose from my bed and opened the window. The air was so fresh that I stayed put. Her footsteps caught my ear first. Maria, the huntress. She always moved like a lioness on the prowl. He arrived shortly after. A bold step, so sure of his right to claim his ground."

Rex built out the picture in his mind's eye.

"They spoke in low tones. I struggled to make out the words. She hissed at him. He growled in return. She said something."

"In Italian?" Dora asked.

"No, in English. I'm almost certain she said the word pay. There was a scuffle of feet. A strangled cry. Then the brush of fabric across the pavement. Only one set of footsteps walked away. His."

Rex's shoulders shook as a shudder ran the length of his spine. It was the stuff of nightmares.

Dora and Clark were equally shaken.

Giovanni broke their trance. "Basta, Mamma. That story is terribile!"

"It is the verita," she countered. "I called out, but my voice was too weak to attract attention. When I learned she'd died, I told the Carabinieri what happened. They believed me, and now you are here. I have done my part to honour her memory. La povera, povera ragazza."

Poor young girl, indeed. Rex cleared his throat. "Did you know her?"

Signora Varotti nodded. "A little. She liked to sit at the table out front and watch across the street. She never told me why, but it wasn't hard to guess. Each time the ambassador's motorcar drove past, she held her breath."

"One last question," Dora said before they left. "When you spoke with her, did you believe her to be Italian?"

The old woman shook her head. "She had an excellent command of the Italian language, but my ear can tell the difference between a native speaker and a foreigner. That said, she was very good. Almost as good at hiding her origin as you."

Clark studied Dora until Rex tapped his hand and shook his head. "Our Theodora is a chameleon, Signora Varotti. Only a very lucky few get a peek at the real woman hiding underneath."

Signora Varotti graced them with another of her bright smiles, but it soon dimmed. "So, too, was Maria. You must take great care that the ambassador doesn't snuff out your light."

Chapter 10
Meet Mary Hunter

Dora sat in the front seat of the car on their way home. She was in no mood to chat with the men, or engage in idle speculation about what they'd learned. A puzzle this complex required the help of her trusted companions, Inga and Harris.

Nonna Matilda answered the door and ushered them inside.

"Are Inga and Harris here?" Dora asked. When Matilda confirmed their presence, Dora dared to request a slight delay to the dinner hour. Although the woman had always shown a remarkable flexibility when it came to serving her guests, meal times were usually sacred. Desperate times, however, called for bravery.

"Certo, Theodora!" Nonna Matilda exclaimed blithely, looking unconcerned.

"I already asked her to push back the dinner bell," Inga explained. "You were gone longer than expected. I presumed you'd want to review your findings before we sit down to eat."

Dora gave Inga a hug. "Never leave my side, you darling girl. I'd be utterly lost without you."

Inga extricated herself from Dora's tight grip and then stepped back with a contemplative expression twisting her lips.

"Wait a minute," Dora said, studying her friend more closely. "Are you planning to leave?"

"Oh no, I was aware from the start that this was a life sentence. I was casting my mind back to see if I could remember what I'd done to earn it."

Dora wrinkled her nose at her friend's cheeky remark. Rex and Clark, who'd come in behind her, chuckled at the women's exchange.

Clark circled around and gave Inga a commiserating pat on the shoulder. "As far as prisons go, at least this one is a gilded cage."

Dora intervened before they got even further off track. "Since we're on the topic of life sentences, might we switch over to discussing our current case?"

"Of course. Harris is waiting in the drawing room with pen, paper, and cocktails," Inga replied.

The group moved to the appointed room, collecting a drink before they chose their seats. Dora and Rex opted for a two-seater sofa, as was their normal preference. Harris and Inga each chose a wingback. Clark stretched his legs across a chaise longue and sighed with relief to be off his feet.

Dora tapped her nails against the side of her glass to get everyone's attention. "Harris and Inga, I assume you two read the police file while we were out, so I won't recount those details. Instead, we'll add some colour commentary based on what we learned."

"Was Sir Francis more forthcoming this time?" Harris asked.

"Thanks to a generous pour of laudanum, the only conversation he was having was with his pillow. Instead, we spoke with Prudence Adams. She's his houseguest."

Inga scrunched her brow but came up short. "The name is vaguely familiar, but I can't place her."

"I had a hard time as well. You'd recognise her face if you saw her. She's a cousin of Lady Emily, Sir Francis's wife. It's her first trip to Rome, and her host stands accused of murder. Needless to say, she isn't having the best experience. We should invite her over."

Inga crossed her arms and eyed Dora. "Why?"

"I'm curious about her." Dora stared off into the mid-distance, gathering her thoughts. "The few times I've spotted her at parties, she's been watching the crowd. I suspect she sees a lot more than she lets on. If Sir Francis has had problems with anyone, he may have mentioned it to her."

Her explanation satisfied Inga. "Very well, we'll keep our eyes peeled for an opportunity to speak further with her. As for today, did she tell you anything relevant to our current case?"

"Yes. She confirmed their piano had recently been tuned. She also mentioned that the ambassador was involved in a private meeting at that time. She could not think of any other opportunities where the ambassador and the victim's paths might have crossed."

"Did she express any opinion about the matter of his guilt or innocence?" Harris asked.

"Innocent, of course. She claimed he wouldn't even know where to find the key to his front door. He never leaves home without an entourage in tow."

Inga grimaced. "That must get annoying after a while — never having a moment to himself."

Clark scoffed. "Sir Francis lives like the kings of old. Everything he does is important, and his so-called retainers should count themselves blessed to be in his presence."

"I take back my earlier lament," Inga said, raising her glass to

Dora. "It seems there are fates worse than having the threads of my life intertwine with yours."

Dora picked up the paper and pen and handed them to Inga.

"Could I get that in writing?"

"Absolutely not. However, I will keep notes for us." Inga's hand glided over the page as she noted their findings thus far. "Anything else to report?"

Dora finished the last of her drink and then set the glass aside. "Yes, one more thing. We spoke with the eyewitness."

"Eyewitness or earwitness?" Inga asked without missing a beat.

Rex spluttered. "Was I the only one to have missed the detail that the witness is blind?"

Clark and Harris shook their heads.

"Inga had to translate for me," Harris said. "To say I was stunned is a vast understatement. What did you learn?"

Instead of answering, Dora ceded the floor to Rex. "I'm interested in hearing your thoughts."

Rex set his drink aside. He leaned forward, resting both hands on his legs before lifting one to prop up his chin. He got a faraway look in his eyes as he replayed the scene.

"I'll start by saying she was more convincing than I expected. Despite having been blind since birth, she painted a vivid picture of the events on that night."

"Do you think someone put her up to it? Perhaps gave her all the information so she could make you believe she really witnessed it?" Harris asked.

Rex didn't have a ready answer to that.

Clark did. "No, and I'll explain why. Everything she described was based in sound. Close your eyes and think back on what she said. She spoke of footsteps, voices, and scrapes. A sighted person wouldn't have thought to do that."

Privately, Dora agreed with Clark, but that didn't mean Signora Varotti had correctly interpreted the scene.

"Something is bothering you," Inga said, looking at Dora.

"You know me so well. Signora Varotti said she'd gone to her window to get some air in the middle of the night. She lives across the street from the murder scene, a quiet side street," Dora added. "I'm willing to admit it is possible she overheard the crime. But at no point did she claim the people involved said their names."

Inga glanced up from her page of notes. "How did Signora Varotti identify them?"

"She said the woman often sat at the table in front of the Varotti family cafe and watched the ambassador's home. Whether their interactions were enough for her to identify the woman by sound alone? Maybe..."

"But not the ambassador," Rex said, jolting upright. "I can't imagine the man ever visited the cafe. It was far too rustic to meet his standards."

"And he never ventures out alone," Clark chimed in. "So why would Signora Varotti be so sure he was the man?"

"You don't think it is possible that the victim said his name?" Harris ventured.

"That only proves his name came up during their discussions. But if Dora and I talk about Rex, it doesn't mean he's there, too."

Rex glanced at his friend. "Why are you and Dora talking about me when I'm not there?"

Dora reached over and caressed his cheek. "Because you are the sun in our sky, darling."

Inga huffed and shook her head in dismay. "Save the platitudes until after we've solved this mystery. Where were we?"

"We were looking at the witness testimony from a new

angle," Harris supplied. "Based on all you've said, I'm willing to mark a few points as fact. First, our victim was definitely interested in something or someone associated with the ambassador's home. She must have since she staked out the scene from the cafe across the street."

Inga's pen scratched across the page as she updated their notes.

"Second, our witness is correct on at least one point. Maria Cacciatore was there on the night in question. She most definitely met someone."

Clark scowled at Harris, looking decidedly unimpressed. "That point was obvious."

"Of course it was. The victim and location of the crime often are. It still behoves us not to lose sight of them."

"Any other facts to add?" Inga asked.

"We don't know this for certain, but I'm willing to bet that Maria didn't choose that meeting point at random. It wasn't exactly convenient to her home address. She had to have been meeting someone from the ambassador's home."

No one contradicted him. Inga turned her page over and made a new list. "I'll add it, but until we can prove this, I suggest we keep our facts separate from our conjecture."

Nonna Matilda entered to announce dinner was served. The group filed into the dining room and seated themselves around the table.

Nonna Matilda ran a tight ship and employed only a minimum number of servants. With no team of footmen to ferry dishes up and down from the kitchen, she served the meals family style.

The centre of the table held an array of dishes. There were cold salads of ripe red tomatoes and glistening white balls of fresh mozzarella. A large ceramic bowl festooned with painted vines held a mountain of spaghetti. Heavy bakeware offered steaming lasagna and melanzane alla parmigiana.

The group didn't stand on ceremony. They passed plates around the table, heaping on spoonfuls of the nearest dish, until no space was left.

Over dinner, they discussed what to do next.

"We need to know more about the victim," Dora said between bites. "Maria Cacciatore — that must be a fake name."

"Caledonia recalled her going by Mary when she saw her in England," Rex said. "Mary... Maria. That makes logical sense. Did she do something similar to her surname? Maria Cacciatore would be Mary Hunter in English."

Dora turned to Clark. "Could you send a telegram to Lord Audley to see if he can look into this back in England?"

Clark stopped with his fork halfway to his mouth. "Lord Audley? The man terrifies me. Do you really think he'll help?"

Dora was certain he would, but she could hardly explain why. Still, the question required an answer.

"He owes us a favour after getting us into the mess with Prince Bertie. You can sign the telegram with Rex's name if you are worried."

Happy with that suggestion, Clark returned to eating.

"I'll have another word with my sister," Rex offered. "I'm also curious about whether it is unusual for a woman to work as a tuner."

"Do you want me to come with you?"

Rex glanced over at Dora in surprise. "I hadn't thought about it, but yes. It would be good for the three of us to spend some time together."

"You can ride over with us. Harris and I arranged to spend the day with Edith. We're going for a drive into the countryside. There is a monastery up in the hills I've been meaning to visit."

"While you're all out, I can make another round of the

social circuit," Clark offered. "After I send the telegram, of course."

Dora lifted her glass of Chianti and proposed a toast. "To well-laid plans and an unstoppable team."

"Hear, hear," the others agreed.

Chapter 11
A Fickle Fear

Rex hurried down the stairs, chastising himself for losing track of time. He launched into apology when he spotted Inga tapping her toe by the front door.

"I got caught up in the police files."

"Find anything interesting?" Harris asked, coming around the corner with a picnic basket in hand.

"My only discovery was how woefully lacking my command of the Italian language is." Rex sighed heavily. "Given our adventures to date, I should have focused my studies on technical terms and crime scene descriptions rather than basic conversation."

Inga unbent long enough to grace Rex with a sympathetic grin. "Chin up, Rex. Full immersion is the best way to master a foreign tongue. By the time we leave, you'll be prepared to speak on any subject. For now, however, I suggest you polish up your apologies as we're going to be late picking up your grandmother."

"Where's Dora," Harris asked, peering up the stairs.

"She left already," Rex explained. "Said she wanted to speak with Grandmama in private."

"She wanted to strategise with Edith about how to best approach Caledonia," Inga added. "On my recommendation, obviously. There's no reason for you two to fumble around in the dark when you have a perfectly good resource to hand. Edith will provide excellent guidance on how Dora and Caledonia can get off on the right foot."

Rex spent the brief car ride hoping Inga was correct. He'd offered to accompany Dora, but she'd waved him off. He trusted both her and his grandmother implicitly, but that didn't stop him from wanting to be in on the plan. Thanks to his own tardiness, that was now impossible.

"Wait in the car. I'll send Grandmama out," Rex said when the driver pulled to a stop in front of the house. He reined in his nerves as he approached the entrance. He'd lost his control with Caledonia during the first conversation. This time had to go better.

His grandmother and Dora were waiting for him in the foyer. Unlike Rex, Edith was calm and collected, showing no concern for his late arrival.

The older woman kissed him on both cheeks, adopting the Italian way of greeting friends and family. "I imagine we'll be out most of the day. I've already told Dora that you're welcome to stay for lunch. Caledonia's lessons with her tutor aren't until later in the afternoon."

Rex tensed as the weight of responsibility landed on his shoulders. "Do we need to get Caledonia to her lesson? What time does it start and where is it?"

Dora laid a hand on his arm. "She isn't a child, darling. I'm sure she'll tell us if she needs a ride."

"Just so," Rex's grandmother agreed. "I've given her as much freedom as I can while here. She'll be off on her own before long and I intend for her to be self-sufficient."

On her own? Rex's eyes bulged. Was his grandmother mad?

Dora leaned close and whispered a reminder. "At her age, I was already a nurse at the front lines. At least your sister isn't dealing with flying bullets and bloodstains on her pinny."

Dora's words had the opposite effect from what she'd intended.

Dora was, well, Dora. She'd never been a typical child. Rex's sister was different.

At the honk of a horn outside, Edith told them goodbye. "Make yourselves at home, and I'll see you both later."

As she marched out the door, Rex noted she was wearing a sensible travel costume. It was only when she turned back to wave goodbye that Rex realised her skirt was actually a pair of wide-leg trousers.

Rex pinched his hand to make sure he was awake. The sharp pain said yes, but his mind balked, nonetheless.

"Come along, darling," Dora said, taking him by the arm. "Caledonia is waiting for us in the music room."

Indeed, his sister sat at the piano. Her pale blonde hair swayed as her head bobbed to the music. Rex found himself singing along to the melody of *La Donna è Mobile* from Verdi's *Rigoletto*.

The catchy tune lifted his spirits, but his mood soured when he recalled the meaning of the words. Was it sheer chance that she was playing a song about the fickleness of women? Or had she chosen the tune to send a message?

There was only one way to find out. He and Dora lingered in the doorway, waiting until she got to the end, to clap their hands.

Caledonia blushed and shifted awkwardly under his praise. "You flatter me. This aria is simple enough that even I can master it."

"You've far surpassed my own abilities," Dora said as she

made her way into the room. "My tutors would have cheered had I even half your talent. Instead, most of my efforts left them in tears. And not the good kind," she added.

Caledonia's eyes shot wide open. She goggled at Dora from across the length of the grand piano. "You had music lessons?"

"Music, singing, sewing, dancing, and guidance on how to hold a conversation with a proper young man. The singing and dancing I enjoyed, music I despaired, and it's best we let the sewing lie. I mastered it eventually, but only after a very unusual sort of lesson."

Caledonia tilted her head to the side and studied Dora as though she were an insect under a microscope.

Rex remembered his first encounters with Dora. She was a puzzle. Each piece of information brought one closer to a solution. But without knowing what the final picture revealed, one had no idea how to assemble them. Caledonia was equally perplexed.

"May we sit?" Rex asked, pointing toward the sitting area.

Caledonia nodded. She pushed her sheet music back into a stack, closed the piano lid, and joined them.

Rex chose the sofa. He expected Dora to sit beside him, but she opted for a chair. Caledonia sat across from Dora.

Instead of being in charge, Rex felt like a referee for a tennis match. His stomach clenched when he realised he had to let the women play it out.

Dora sat upright. She rested her arms on the armrest and left her legs uncrossed, her body language communicating openness.

Caledonia was her opposite. She crossed her ankles and tucked her legs tight against the chair legs. She fidgeted with her hands and then clutched them together so she'd stop.

Rex would bet money that Caledonia was as nervous as he

was. That warmed his spirits. She cared about his and Dora's opinions.

There was hope yet that they'd find a way through.

Dora broke the silence. "Caledonia, we need your help. We must ask you questions, and we're depending upon you to answer."

Caledonia's fingers clenched. "I will do my best to aid you. I understand the seriousness of the situation."

Dora continued on, "Open and honest conversations require a two-way street. I cannot in good conscience ask questions of you if I am not willing to answer yours in return. In your shoes, my list would be endless."

Caledonia and Rex both shifted forward in their seats.

Dora remained as poised as always. "Rex told you about our marriage. That makes you and me sisters. Although I've never had a sister, I do have two brothers. One never came home from the war. The other I didn't see for nearly half a decade. My secrets, such as they were, drove a wedge between us. Even now, we are still rebuilding our relationship."

"Dora..." Rex murmured. Didn't she realise how much she was revealing?

Dora held up a hand to stop him. She held his gaze for a long moment, letting her calm demeanour communicate what words could not. Trust her. There was nothing to fear.

Rex settled back in his chair, ceding the floor once again.

Dora shifted her attention back to the young woman sitting across from her. "I am sure the news of our marriage raised concerns. Who is Theodora Laurent? Am I a fortune-hunter? Is my dedication to your brother real? There is only one way for me to put your concerns to rest."

"You will tell me who you are?" Caledonia's voice shook with emotion.

"Indeed. I'll start with my name. My parents christened me Dorothy Jane Cavendish."

"Cavendish?" Caledonia cocked her head to the side while she worked out why that name was familiar.

Dora had no intention of making Caledonia fill in the blanks with guesses. "I am the only daughter of Stephen and Adaline Cavendish. Your grandmother knows them as the Duke and Duchess of Dorset."

Caledonia's eyes widened, and she gasped, "But that would make you—"

"Lady Dorothy." Dora wrinkled her nose. "I disliked my name so much that I refused to answer to anything other than Dora. I was a miscreant from the day I was born. My parents sent me to a Swiss finishing school in my teens. I ran away to join the war effort. It was there that I met Inga and your brother."

Caledonia's head spun in Rex's direction. "You've known her this long and never let on?"

"Oh no! She had me fooled, just like everyone else. Remember when I got injured while out on a mission? The man I accompanied — the man who died that day —was Dora's first husband."

"He was a dear friend, and it was a marriage of convenience," Dora hastened to add. "He died the day after our wedding, after a traitor sold out his whereabouts. I had to get justice for him. That was my first foray into the world of intrigue," Dora explained. "I worked in the shadows. Rex had no idea I was there. After that, I was hooked."

"When did you stop?" Caledonia asked.

"I haven't," Dora replied. "I still work on behalf of the government. Rex does, too. This information is top secret. We've told no one outside of our immediate families, and the people in my household. Lord Clark is in the dark. You cannot discuss this."

Caledonia paled, but she nodded her understanding. She looked at Rex. "Your comment makes sense now, the one where you said Dora's identity was worth more than her life."

"My life depends on keeping many secrets, including our marriage. I am only effective so long as I appear to have no long-term allegiances to anyone or any place."

Caledonia gave her words careful consideration. Her eyes flicked back and forth as she put more puzzle pieces into place. "What about now? This case with Sir Francis."

"Officially, Rex and Clark are tasked with ferreting out the truth. I met Sir Francis several years ago. When you put those two things together, they provide excuse enough for me to be involved."

"Blimey!" Caledonia fell back in her seat. She marvelled at the pair. "My own brother is a spy. Wait! Have you told Mother and Father?"

"No," Rex hurried to reply. "Only Grandmama. She can tell them should the necessity ever arise."

"That's smart of you," Caledonia agreed. "They'd never understand. They pay no attention to things beyond the boundaries of our estate. They can't imagine why anyone would ever need to range farther."

Caledonia's remark showed an astute understanding of the family dynamics. Her presence in Rome suggested she had more in common with Rex than with the rest of their family. That raised a question about her own plans for the future.

"What about you?" Rex asked. "Do you intend to return home soon?"

Caledonia waved her hands while shaking her head. "The only thing Mother wants to discuss is eligible bachelors in the neighbouring counties. I had to beg Grandmama to save me.

She came up with the excuse of visiting Rome and told Mother and Father. They couldn't refuse her. They are too scared."

Dora chuckled. "Them and anyone else in high society with half a brain. Your grandmother is not someone to cross. What of you and these lessons? Are you truly interested in music?"

"Absolutely," the young woman answered without hesitation. "I wrote to Maestro Mantovani as soon as Grandmama suggested we travel abroad. He agreed to take me on."

"That brings us full circle to why we are here." Dora glanced at Rex. "Would you like to take over now?"

"I will, but only to give you a break from talking. Caledonia, have you given any more thought to the investigation? Perhaps you've recalled something more about the woman?"

Caledonia's shoulders sank. "I have searched my memory time and again. I'm positive she is the same woman I saw in England."

"Could we contact the event organisers? Might they have a list of the attendees?"

Caledonia considered her brother's question. "I can write to them and ask, but I'd have to include a photograph. Do you know how many English girls have the name Mary?"

Dora pulled a face, and Rex flinched. Caledonia made a good point.

"Besides that, I'm not sure she worked for the organisers. She might as easily have been someone's assistant."

Until then, Rex had assumed that Mary had been a performer. The alternative made more sense, especially given her current occupation. He raised this with his sister. "Are there many women working in the music industry? Beyond teaching piano lessons, I mean."

"More than you would imagine. Women often employ other

women. Take Dora for example. She chose to travel with Inga instead of a man for a reason."

"But Dora is unique," Rex argued, missing the point.

"I am, in so many ways," Dora agreed. "This, however, isn't one of them. Having a female assistant makes travel and accommodation simpler."

"What about now? Mary arrived here within the last few months. Tuning pianos is manual labour, even if it does require a specific skill set. Are there many female tuners?"

Caledonia took her time answering. "It's uncommon, but not impossible, if she had a good reason. It would help to know why she came to Italy in the first place. If she was travelling with someone else and got dismissed, it would explain much. Under those circumstances, she'd have been desperate to find any work. Maybe she was looking for a way to get back home. Could that have been why she contacted someone at the embassy?"

Rex looked at Dora. She shrugged her shoulders. As always, every conversation raised more questions than answers.

Caledonia stood and went over to the piano. She picked up a card and brought it to Rex. "This is the shop we contacted for the tuning service."

Rex glanced at the card and recognised the name as the same one listed in the police files. He thanked his sister and pocketed the card.

"Any other questions for me?" his sister asked.

"None for now," he replied.

Caledonia sat back down again and looked at Dora. "In that case, can I ask more about you?"

"Absolutely! For you, my new sister, my life is an open book."

The pair launched into an enthusiastic conversation. Some of the stress of the last few days rolled from Rex's shoulders.

Despite the lack of warning and a rough start, his and Dora's relationship with Caledonia was blossoming.

He hoped their luck held. They desperately needed the owner of the piano store to provide answers to the ever-growing pile of questions.

Chapter 12
Behind the Ivory Keys

After a simple lunch of pasta followed by bowls of pistachio gelato, Caledonia stood to gather her things.

"I'm sorry to rush out, but if I don't leave now, I won't make it to my lesson on time. The maestro is a stickler for timeliness."

"Really?" Dora gave Caledonia a closer look. "Most Italians view time as a fluid entity."

"I didn't say the maestro himself would be there on time. Just that he expects me to be waiting when he does arrives." Caledonia rolled her eyes, making both Dora and Rex laugh.

"Do you want a ride there?" Rex asked.

"Our driver will take me," Caledonia assured him. She turned to leave the dining room, but spun back before she reached the doorway. "On second thought, perhaps I should ride with you. The maestro is at the centre of the music scene. He might be able to help."

While Rex went to telephone their driver, Dora sidled closer to Caledonia. "Tell me about this maestro of yours. Is he handsome? Witty?"

Caledonia pulled a face. When she answered, her tone was

laced with disgust. "He's older than my father and has hair growing in his nose and ears!"

Dora giggled at the resulting picture. She'd missed the mark with that question. Still, she pressed on. Caledonia's attention to, or lack thereof, in potential love interests would tell her a lot. It was one thing to turn her nose up at a man promoted by her parents. It was quite another to resist the attentions of Italy's Romeos.

"No one else, then? Another student or the assistant?"

Caledonia gave Dora a bland look. She was not amused. "I'm not closed off to the idea of love and marriage eventually, but I'm not yet twenty. I've no desire to cede control over my life to some man."

Dora tweaked her nose. "What if he hands control over to you?"

That caught Caledonia's attention for a moment, but soon enough she was shaking her head.. "No, still not interested."

"Not interested in what?" Rex asked, coming up behind them.

"Stepping out...with a man," Dora replied. She fluttered her eyelashes at him, playing the innocent.

Rex's stomach lurched at the idea of his baby sister on the arm of... well, anyone. "I should think not!"

Caledonia huffed at her brother's emphatic statement. "See? What did I tell you? They all want control." She marched off, leaving Rex spluttering behind her.

Dora placated Rex and soon enough, they were on their way. The maestro worked out of a studio near the Impresa Costanzi, the home of Rome's opera scene.

After five minutes spent cooling their heels, Maestro Mantovani burst through the studio door. Watching him glide across the room shaped Dora's opinion of the man.

It was more appropriate to say that he entered stage right,

fully embodying his role as a musical virtuoso. His silver hair, styled in a pompadour, shone under the electric lights of the studio. From his prominent nose to his broad shoulders and on down to his expansive waistline, the man commanded attention. Even his movements were exaggerated enough to be clear to those seated in the back row.

Dora was rarely upstaged, but Maestro Mantovani made her feel like a chorus girl waiting in the stage wings.

Dora liked him immediately.

Caledonia bobbed her head in greeting and hurried to take her seat on the piano bench.

Another man had followed in the Maestro's wake. He was rail thin, with long arms and legs. His oversized feet gave him the appearance of a puppy. However, he lacked the creature's rambunctious spirit. There was a sombre cast to his features that turned to reverence when he opened his violin case.

"Signorina Caledonia, have you brought us guests?" the maestro asked.

"My brother, Lord Rex, and his companion, Miss Theodora Laurent."

The maestro welcomed them with open arms. "Have you come to listen in on your sister's lesson? If so, I must warn you that with her, I have taken an unusual approach."

"Caledonia explained why she is here. As much as we'd love to stay, I'm afraid we can only linger long enough to ask you a question," Rex said.

"Eh?" the maestro raised his bushy brows. "Certo. Ask me anything."

"What can you tell us about the reputation of Pianoforti Ennio?" Rex asked, giving the name of the piano shop where Mary had worked.

The maestro's expression smoothed. He pointed to the

piano that Caledonia was to play. "This beautiful instrument comes from Ennio. He is the only one I trust here in Rome."

"Because he has access to the best?" Dora asked.

"In part, but also because his eye for quality is second to none.. Anyone can stock the newest models, signora. It takes a trained eye to see past the surface shine. Take Antonio here." Maestro Mantovani pointed at the young man. "He failed audition after audition because of stage fright. His teacher came to me and explained. I snuck into his lesson and listened from the hallway."

Maestro Mantovani's eyes shone with tears. "It was musica such as I have not heard in a generation. Together with his teacher, we came up with a way to make him grow comfortable with me. Then next, the stage. In a few years, when he is ready, he will bring the audience to their feet. Ennio is the same. His true talent lies in restoration. That is why people hire him to care for their pianoforte."

When a few more questions revealed little new information, Rex thanked the maestro for allowing their interruption. Rex and Dora left them to get on with the lesson.

"He made quite an impression," Rex admitted when they were back in the car.

"As does your sister. You never hinted that she was a child prodigy." Dora glanced at Rex. "I take it you didn't know."

"I hadn't a clue. Now I'm wondering what else I've missed about my family."

"I don't suggest you go digging for information on your grandmother. It might look like a treasure trove on the outside, but open that lid and you'll discover Pandora was the original owner."

Rex barked a laugh. "You've nothing to fear on that point. No one is foolish enough to venture into Grandmama's domain."

The pair settled into a companionable silence as their driver battled the Roman traffic. Slowly, the buildings grew larger and farther apart as they worked their way from the historic centre.

Pianoforti Ennio's location in an industrial area made sense now that they knew his specialty. Here, away from the ancient ruins for which Rome was famous, one could gain deeper insight into Italy's more modern ambitions. Many of the factories they passed were new. Bicycles and motorcars filled the spaces in between the buildings, giving an indication of the vast numbers of workers inside.

With Mussolini at the helm of the nation, there was a renewed focus on growth and employment. He was intent on Italy becoming a superpower so that what happened to the country at the end of the Great War would not be repeated.

England's history was littered with examples of allies becoming enemies before going back to friends again. It remained to be seen on which side of the line Italy would fall. Dora had yet to form an opinion on the matter. There was still much to be explored, but only after the situation with the ambassador was resolved.

Pianoforte Ennio occupied one of the older buildings in the area. A simple wooden sign bearing the company name and the image of a grand piano hung above the door. The driver let them out before pulling off to the side to wait.

Inside was a mid-sized workshop. Dora counted six men working on various tasks in the room. Each station held a musical instrument in varying stages of assembly. Tools hung from pegboards and the floor was swept clean.

Her gaze came to rest on an older man near the back of the room. His thick moustache and beard were sprinkled with white hair and his portly frame leaned against a piano. He'd fixed his attention on whatever he was doing to the piano strings. Based on his age and the way the younger employee watched him with respect, Dora presumed he must be Ennio.

Dora and Rex waited patiently until Ennio finished his task. When he straightened up, he seemed surprised to find he had visitors. He grabbed a nearby rag and wiped his hands clean before hurrying over.

"Buongiorno, signori. Come posso aiutarvi?" he asked.

Dora chose her words carefully. She didn't want any language barrier to stand in the way. Over the years, she'd learned that people expressed more emotion in their native tongue. Hunting for the right words often held one back.

"Are you Signore Ennio Campanelli?" she asked in Italian. After he nodded, she explained, "I believe one of your employees tuned our piano. It is in the home of the Dowager Duchess of Rockingham."

Ennio's shoulders tensed. "Is there a problem with it?"

"No, not at all," Dora rushed to add. "This is about your tuner — Maria Cacciatore. Lord Rex and I are searching for the truth about what happened to her."

The tension in Ennio's shoulders bled out, being replaced by a weary expression on his face. "Povera Maria! I will help in any way that I can. Let's go to my office."

He led Dora and Rex into a narrow room tucked into the rear of the shop. Like the workshop, the office was tidy. A single, open ledger sat on the desk. Others lined a shelf built into the wall. Framed photographs decorated another wall. In each, Ennio stood with a musician. Dora recognised her favourite jazz pianist in one of them, lending further credence to his reputation as a master of his trade.

The old man bade them to sit in the visitor's chairs while he sat behind the desk. "Are you from the British embassy?" he asked.

"We are here on behalf of the British government," Rex replied. "We have no direct ties to the embassy. We have reason to believe Maria Cacciatore was actually a British citizen named Mary. Would you know anything about this?"

"I can't speak to her real name, but I had my suspicions. She was highly guarded about her background.

"But yet, you hired her to work on your behalf."

Ennio shrugged. "What can I say? I have a granddaughter named Mariangela. She is younger, but headstrong. Maria, or Mary, as you call her, reminded me of her." He leaned over the desk and lowered his voice. "I feared Mary had found herself in a difficult situation. When she showed up here, she was desperate for work of any kind. She said music was the only thing she knew."

"Why didn't she teach lessons?" Dora asked.

"That was my first suggestion. All she would tell me was that she couldn't bear to be dependent on the whims of a single person again. I explained it did not have to be that way - that she could have several students." He stopped and shook his head. "As hard-headed as my Maria."

"Did you train her to repair pianos? How long did she work here?"

"She demonstrated her capabilities, which is the only reason I allowed her to visit our clients. I have a reputation to uphold. With a few tips from me, she was more than capable. All in all, she was with us for two, almost three months."

"You never had any complaints about her work?" Dora asked.

"Never!" Ennio's reply was forceful. "As I said, my livelihood depends on the trust of my clients. I'd never have kept her on if someone did."

"Even though she reminded you of your granddaughter?" Rex raised his eyebrows to show his scepticism.

Ennio pointed toward the workshop. "None of the men out there are related to me. There is a reason I don't hire family. My son, he thought this would be an easy job. He could coast on my legacy. I soon disabused him of that notion. Now, he works at a factory down the road. A desk job," he said with a sneer.

Dora placated him with a sympathetic smile. "Is there anything else you can tell us? She must have a family somewhere. They deserve to know what happened to her."

Dora's play on the old man's sympathies did the trick. He opened a drawer in a desk and flipped through his files. He found the right one and passed it to Dora. "This is everything I had on her. The Carabinieri told me her documents were fake. Maybe you will see something they didn't. A record of her client visits is also inside."

Dora took the file and promised to return it to him when they were done.

"There is no need. The relevant information is already in each client's record. There is no more I can do for povera Mary." He went silent for a moment, his gaze fixed on the folder while his eyes blinked back a tear. When he spoke again, his voice was rough with emotion. "If you find her family, tell them she was a good girl and will be missed."

His words caused Dora's throat to close tight. Without Inga, Harris, and now Rex to keep an eye on her, she might have met a similar end.

Dead, in an unmarked grave, and her family none the wiser.

Dora reached across the desk and took Ennio's scarred hand in her own. She squeezed it tight. "I give you my word, Signore Campanelli, that her death will not go unavenged."

Even if that meant taking down a fellow countryman.

Chapter 13
The Undercover Officer

Rex and Dora returned to an empty home. Inga and Harris dined with Edith. Clark had accepted an invitation with other friends. Nonna Matilda took it upon herself to arrange an intimate dinner for two on the garden terrace. The roses climbing the trellis perfumed the air. For a moment in time, the newlyweds set aside their worries and fears and simply enjoyed the company of one another.

Not long after the sun disappeared from the horizon and the first stars twinkled in the sky, the rest of their group returned. Nonna Matilda brought out a tray bearing glasses of limoncello. After Clark, Inga, and Harris sat down, they raised their glasses in a silent toast and then sipped the tart liquor.

"Now that you are all here, we should update you on what we discovered. We paid a visit to our victim's employer." Rex set his glass aside and recounted their day.

When he finished, Harris opened his notepad to his page of facts about the case. "Every bit helps us get a better picture of Mary. Based on what you learned, we can add that Mary hid her real identity, and went to great lengths to ensure this. She also desired a job where she could move around each day." He looked up. "Was this because she wanted access to multiple homes, or because she was waiting for her chance to visit the embassy?"

"You don't think she told her employer the truth?" Inga asked. "It isn't farfetched that a young woman, on her own in a foreign country, could end up in a dangerous situation."

Silence fell over the group as they all considered Inga's point. It was a rare case where Rex didn't trust his instincts. Sure, he'd heard stories of entitled men taking advantage of their positions to compromise their servants. But those stories had always been second or third hand.

He glanced at Clark, and his friend shrugged when their eyes met. He, too, had no experience with the trials and tribulations of life as a working woman.

It fell to Dora to reply. "Such things happen. The women in those usually end up fearful. They want a refuge, not to be sent gallivanting about town. And especially not in a foreign country."

"I agree," Harris said. "If Mary wanted a safe space, she'd have begged Ennio to employ her in his workshop. She made that request for a reason. When we figure out what it was, we'll know why she is dead."

Inga levelled a glare at her husband. "That's been the case since we started. You'd think by now we'd have made more progress."

Harris was unruffled by her words. Although she'd flung them at him, he wasn't the real source of her frustration. In the middle of an investigation, they all became prickly.

Dora intervened to get them back on track. "Nothing for us but to ask more questions. We've got a list of the homes she visited on behalf of the piano shop. It reads like a who's who of the expat community."

Clark took the list from Dora. "No Italians?"

"Ennio said he sent her to his English clients, where her language skills would be best put to use."

Clark scanned the list, and a broad smile crossed his face. "How would you like to question most of these people in a single night?"

"Let me guess," Rex said. "You got word of a social event."

"Word and invitations. Both the Italian King and Prime Minister are on the guest list. If all three of us go, we can work our way around the room."

Rex found no fault with the plan. "When is this event?"

"Tomorrow evening," Clark said. He mimed a fake bow. "You're welcome, you're welcome."

Inga leaned over and patted him on the head as though he were a little boy. "Excellent work, deary. You've earned an extra serving of dessert with your dinner tomorrow."

Clark eyed his waistband and groaned. "I never thought I'd say this, but for the first time in my life, dessert doesn't sound appealing."

"Another drink, then?" Inga asked.

Her suggestion met with his approval. Clark stood up and offered to fetch the bottle of limoncello so they could all have another round.

Dora took advantage of his temporary absence to make a suggestion. "I want to visit the address Mary gave to Ennio. I can take Cynthia with me. I promised to show her the sights."

"I'll come along with you," Inga offered. "If you get caught up investigating something, you're likely to forget she's with you. The last thing we need is your lady's maid lost in Rome."

Clark returned with the promised bottle and refilled everyone's glasses. "What's next, then?"

Harris scanned his notepad and then adjusted his view upward. "The ambassador's household. You've yet to interview the staff."

Clark sighed. "That will take hours. But needs must and all that."

Rex had to admit that Clark wasn't cut out for a long day of speaking with servants. He turned to Harris. "Why don't you come along with me?"

Harris reared back. "How will you explain bringing your butler along?"

"Simple. No one here knows you are our butler. You can pretend to be some kind of official. Or perhaps a police officer!"

Given Harris was a retired officer pretending to be a butler, the role wouldn't require much of a stretch of his acting muscles.

Clark was so delighted to have an out that he chimed in his agreement. "If we put you in a staid suit and you add a scowl, I'd believe you worked for the Yard. Anyone would."

Harris squirmed under the collective gaze of the group. "Fine. I'll do it on one condition."

"What's that?" Clark asked.

"You have to find me a boring black suit. I left all of mine in England."

The conversation turned to more pleasant matters as Inga and Harris recounted their adventures in the hills. When they finished, everyone agreed to turn in for the night. They all had a busy day ahead.

* * *

The next morning, Clark made good on his word. Rex spotted a servant delivering a package to Harris. It was too early for most shops to be open, but apparently Clark hadn't let that stand in his way. With Nonna Matilda's help, he'd procured an appropriate ensemble for a police detective on holiday, all with the tags still on.

After breakfast, Rex and Harris took off. Harris drove the

car, explaining that he relished the chance to pit his skills against the Roman drivers.

Rex turned his mind to their task. Their four days in Rome so far had been productive. They'd already retraced the steps of the Carabinieri and discovered at least two new pieces of information about the victim. The Italian police hadn't known that Maria Cacciatore's real name was Mary. As such, they hadn't looked very hard at the Ambassador's household.

With several new strands to investigate, Rex was optimistic about their chances of identifying the killer. He said as much to Harris after the guard waved them through the gate.

"Confidence is a useful tool," Harris agreed as they exited the car. "Often, it is the only thing that sustains you when the investigation hits a brick wall."

Rex readied himself to approach the front door, but stopped when he realised Harris wasn't following. The man had paused next to the car and was surveying the landscape. He slowly turned in a circle as he took in the expansive manicured lawn and impressive villa.

"Thoughts?" Rex asked as he came up beside the man.

"A few. First, if you had all this private land to yourself, why would you hold a secret meeting on the pavement outside?"

"I certainly would not, but most people don't have our training."

"Second, what about the guards at the gate? Are they there at all hours? If so, how did the ambassador get past them?"

"We'll ask the butler. Speaking of, he's watching us through the window. Shall we get a move on?"

Harris swung around in time to see the curtain drop back into place.

The butler answered within moments of Rex ringing the bell. "Can I help you, my lord?"

"Yes, but first allow me to introduce you to my associate.

This is Detective Inspector Harrison. He happens to be in Rome on holiday, so I recruited him to the cause."

The butler shifted his gaze away from Rex and finally deigned to acknowledge Harris. He took in Harris's modest suit and worn black shoes. "Welcome to Italy, Detective Inspector. I take it you wish to speak with the ambassador? He is in a meeting, but you are both welcome to wait. I will let him know you are here."

Rex held up a hand to stop him. "We were hoping to have a word with you, if you can spare the time."

The butler's eyebrows jogged up his forehead. "In that case, please come in."

He guided them to a smaller reception room than Rex had been in before. Rex and Harris took a seat. The butler remained standing, even after Rex invited him to sit.

"It would not be appropriate," he explained.

Rex cut him off. "This is hardly a social call. My neck will end up with a cramp. Please, sit. I insist."

The butler finally sat, but only after choosing the simplest wooden chair in the room. He perched awkwardly, ready to leap to his feet should anyone open the door.

As agreed in advance, Harris took the lead in the questioning.

"We have reason to believe that the victim, Miss Maria Cacciatore, was acquainted with someone inside the home. Can you speak to this matter? As the head of the household staff, I'm sure your practiced eye misses nothing."

The butler preened. "To the best of my knowledge, that woman was only here once. I banned her from the grounds after that occasion."

How was this only now coming to light? Rex steeled himself not to look at Harris.

Harris nodded, giving no hint this was new information. He

took a stab in the dark. "This was the time Miss Cacciatore came to tune the piano?"

"Yes, Detective. Pianoforti Ennio came highly recommended, but I found it strange he sent a young woman. That's why I assigned a footman to monitor her."

"Did something happen during the tuning? I must confess I don't know what is involved in such an undertaking."

"It is also outside my area of expertise. I expected it to be a minor task, half an hour at most. When an hour came and went, I had to call the footman away for another assignment. I checked on her progress. The woman had tools spread out on a cloth and was busy testing the keys. I left her to it," he paused before adding, "and that was my mistake."

"How so?" Rex asked.

The butler glanced at Rex and flushed in embarrassment. Rex thought he might clam up, but Harris encouraged him to be forthright.

"You understand that this is a very busy household, my lord. More so than the average upper class home. Sir Francis uses the residence as both a workplace and a home. In a single day, we might host a meeting with one group, luncheon with another, a private family dinner, and then finish with a ball."

"And yet, you oversee all of this with aplomb." Harris gave the butler a nod of approval. "I understand why you had to leave Miss Cacciatorre on her own. What did she do?"

"She wandered off!" The butler's face reddened in anger. "The sheer cheek! Next time I saw her, she was upstairs. Near the bedrooms," he added, wiggling his eyebrows.

"Was she lost?" Rex glanced upwards, guessing at the floor plan. This was a large house with dozens of rooms. It would be easy to get turned around.

"So lost that she went up the stairs instead of down?" The butler was incredulous. "I frogmarched her out the door. I told her she could explain to her employer why we would no longer be using their services."

"Did she say anything? Offer any excuse?" Harris asked.

"She stuttered in half Italian and half broken English. I paid her no attention. My only regret is that I didn't make her turn out her pockets."

"Why is that?'"

"Because she was a thief! Why else would she have had the ambassador's lapel pin and card, unless she stole them while she was here?"

The butler stood then, too indignant to remain seated. "No one deserves the death she had, but mark my words. She was up to no good, and her deeds caught up with her. Sir Francis is not to blame. Neither is anyone else here."

Rex looked at Harris, who gave him a subtle shake of the head. There was no point in lingering. If Mary was using her visits as a cover for theft, this cast her death in a new light.

Chapter 14
Footloose in Rome

C lark wasn't the only one to avail himself of the local shops. When Dora came down for a late breakfast, she found a large white box waiting by her chair. She verified the contents met her needs before asking the servant for a steaming cappuccino.

Inga was equally curious when she spotted the box a few minutes later. Dora refused to reveal the contents. She pointed at the ceiling to remind Inga that Clark was still there. "I'll explain everything when we meet Cynthia."

After breakfast, the women chose comfortable walking shoes, ensured they'd safely stored their pocket money, and then crossed to the guest house out back. There, they found Cynthia ready to go. Dora's lady's maid had chosen her nicest dress and paired it with shiny new shoes.

"Will I do?" she asked, stepping back so Dora and Inga could have a full-length view.

"No," Dora answered. When Cynthia's chin wobbled, Dora rushed to add, "None of us will. We're going undercover. That's why I sent out for new clothes. Can we change in your room?"

Cynthia was happy to oblige, but Inga was not. "What's wrong with my outfit?"

"I'll explain while we change. Lead the way, Cynthia."

Cynthia led them to a spacious, well-appointed bedroom. She apologised for the state of it, even though there wasn't a single thing out of place. Although her real skill was forgery, she had clearly mastered the duties of a lady's maid.

"Let me explain before I hand you the clothing." Dora motioned for the women to sit. "There is every chance we might be spotted today, especially if we visit the major tourist attractions. Theodora Laurent is known for unorthodox behaviour. However, going out on the town with her lady's maid would be outlandish, even for her. Such an action is bound to raise eyebrows and questions. Therefore, we need to go incognito. That's where these come in."

Dora handed Cynthia and Inga each a dress and then took one for herself.

The fabric was light-weight, cut in a flattering drop waist, and the patterns in different pastel shades.

"We're going as triplets?" Inga asked, glancing at the other two women. "You realise we look nothing alike."

"We're going as a trio of best friends, visiting Rome together. You know the type I mean-matching dresses bought on holiday, sunglasses, and lots of whispering and secrets."

Inga shuddered. Dora smirked at her predictable reaction.

Cynthia was thrilled with the plan. Dora cajoled Inga into going along with it. After they'd all changed clothes, Cynthia set off to find a comfortable pair of shoes.

Dora asked Inga to help her don her brunette wig. Inga lent a hand, but grumbled under her breath the whole time.

"Chin up, dear," Dora said when she caught Inga's eye in the mirror. "Think of this as us catching up on an activity the war stole from us. Had we lived ordinary lives in ordinary times, we might have done this years ago."

"Sightseeing with friends? Yes. Wearing this shade of peach? Absolutely not!"

"Give the dress to Cynthia after we're done. She, at least, showed the proper amount of appreciation for my gift."

"That's the first sensible suggestion you've made today," Inga replied in a dry tone.

Dressed and disguised, the women got into the car and headed off. Dora gave the driver an address, and they were on their way.

"Our first stop will be the address Mary gave to Ennio. From there, the Colosseum is a short walk."

The driver stopped the car in front of a narrow townhouse. The three women climbed out of the car and gathered on the pavement. Dora took in the surroundings, noting the fruit and vegetable stand two doors down and another of Rome's ubiquitous cafes across the street. From the shouts of children floating on the breeze, Dora presumed there must be a school nearby. This was a family-friendly neighbourhood. What did that say about Mary's choice to live there? Dora didn't have an answer to that question.

"Shall I do the honours?" Inga asked, motioning toward the door. Dora waved her on. Inga gave a polite trio of knocks and stepped back to stand beside Dora. Cynthia lingered off to the side.

A harried woman opened the door with a baby on her hip and a toddler wrapped around her left leg. If she was surprised to find three strange women standing on her doorstep, she didn't show it.

"We're here about a room you rent," Dora said by way of a beginning.

The woman stopped her there. "We've already rented it out. You're too late."

Dora threw out a hand to prevent the woman from closing the door in her face. "Wait! We aren't here to put in an application. We are looking for the previous tenant. Maria Cacciatorre? She was a friend of ours."

The woman's face softened. "Come inside." She turned heel, expecting Dora and the others to follow behind. She marched along the corridor, paying no mind to the little girl latched onto her leg.

Dora glanced into the rooms as they passed a line of doors. In front was a small reception room, next a study, and then a dining room with seating for eight. The woman of the house didn't stop until she reached a kitchen at the rear of the house. There, she sat the baby in a wooden chair, strapped him in, and popped a dummy in his mouth.

The little girl blinked up at Dora, mesmerised enough by the sight of visitors that she kept quiet.

"You knew Maria?" the woman asked. "I've not seen you before."

Dora had prepared for this discussion. "We met her at a piano concerto. She was so private about where she lived we had to get her address from the Carabinieri."

The woman accepted the explanation. "I don't know why I am questioning you. I should be pleased Maria had any friends at all. For a young woman, she was remarkably quiet. Made for a good tenant, but I worried life was passing her by." She sniffled and her eyes filled with tears.

Dora lowered her lashes. She didn't have to feign her sympathies. No woman's life should be cut short the way Mary's was.

Dora gave the woman a moment to pull herself together before explaining why they were there. "We wanted to send

Maria's family a note expressing our condolences. Did she leave an address for them?"

"I'm not sure. The Carabinieri searched her room. Afterwards, my husband boxed everything up. We donated her clothing and shoes, but her more personal items are still here." The woman paused as a new thought struck. "You could go through them. Although Maria lived here, we barely knew her. I didn't feel right pawing through her things. But you were her friends..."

Dora could hardly believe her luck. "We'd be happy to do that. If we find contact information, we'll forward her belongings to her family."

Before the woman could make a move to retrieve the box, the little girl's patience ran out. She tugged on her mother's dress to get her attention and asked for a biscotto.

"Aspetta, Chiara," her mother scolded. The child wasn't content to wait. She burst into tears, setting the baby off as well. The mother scooped up one child and hurried to reassure the other.

Dora glanced over her shoulder at Inga. There, she found little help. The two of them had no experience with children.

Inga followed suit, turning to see if Cynthia had a solution. Cynthia gave a feverish shake of her head as well.

Meanwhile, the woman was growing increasingly frustrated as neither child demonstrated a willingness to wait. Eventually, she threw her hands in the air, both figuratively and literally.

"You come back later," the woman suggested. "When my husband is home. He can retrieve the box from the attic."

Dora's decided an escape was indeed in order. "Shall we say six? Is that late enough?"

The woman assured her that was fine and asked if they minded seeing themselves out. She didn't have to ask twice.

Outside on the pavement, Dora, Inga, and Cynthia sighed in relief at being away from the madness of young children.

Inga scowled at the doorway, making clear her lack of desire to return. "Do we really need that box? The Carabinieri would have taken anything of interest."

"The police would have only been searching for her identity. Who knows what Mary left behind? Even the smallest clue will help us learn something new about her." Satisfied with her plan, Dora linked arms with Inga and Cynthia. "Come now, ladies, Rome's ancient history awaits."

* * *

Cynthia's wide-eyed enthusiasm restored Dora's spirits. She stared in awe at every statue. When they turned a corner and the Colosseum came into view, she stopped dead in her tracks.

"It's so... solid!" she squealed. "When you said ruins, I assumed there'd be stones littering the ground. But the walls — look how high they soar!"

Dora and Inga exchanged a secret smile.

"Would you like to go inside?"

Cynthia gasped and turned to Dora. "We can?"

"We can and will." Dora had to hurry to keep up with Cynthia. The woman's boundless excitement was infectious. Even Inga softened enough to speed up her steps.

Up close, the Colosseum lost none of its lustre. The arched windows towered over their heads. With a little imagination, they could hear the chants of the ancient Romans encouraging the gladiators in their fights. The clash of swords was so real, Dora would have sworn she stood on the edge of an actual battle.

When they walked around to the other side of the ruins, Dora discovered why. Two men, dressed in full gladiator costumes, faced off with their swords held high. The surrounding crowd cheered them on. Despite the sharp edges and sweaty brows, she had nothing to fear. These men were actors, playing a role for the visiting tourists. Dora dropped a handful of coins into the flat cap lying near the edge of the crowd.

A swarthy man sold them three tickets and then waved them inside the Colosseum gates. Signs hung from walls, telling the stories of the bygone days and the research to discover them. A young man with a bright smile hurried over to meet them.

"Signorine belle! Would you like a tour? I'm a professional," he boasted, holding up an official-looking card. Dora doubted the authenticity of said item, but one glance at Cynthia's face convinced her to play along. Her lady's maid deserved the full experience, and who better to provide it than a local dependent on their tips.

Having visited several times before, Dora waved for Cynthia to walk ahead with their guide, while she and Inga followed in their wake. Dora clutched onto Inga's arm and leaned over to whisper in her ear. "See, I told you our disguises would work. If our guide had the faintest clue who I am, he wouldn't have a minute to spare for our Cynthia."

Inga gave Dora a side-eyed stare. "That sure of your looks, Miss Theodora?"

Dora chuckled and rapped Inga on the arm. "I'm sure my deep pocketbook would be my most appealing feature. This way, Cynthia gets to be the star audience of his one-man show. Let's hurry, though. I'm curious to hear what he has to say."

Cynthia and the guide had reached the inside of the arena. Here, the age of the monument was more evident. Their guide explained that after the fall of the Roman empire, the locals treated the Colosseum as a quarry for their marble needs. It was far easier to haul pieces away than excavate new. Gone were the seating and decorations. The old wooden floor had long since rotted away.

"What's that down there?" Cynthia asked, pointing at the warren of exposed walkways at the Colosseum's lowest level.

"Those are the old underfloor levels. The guards would have used those pathways to bring in the slaves and animals for the infamous fights. I can only imagine how dark and smoky those pathways would have been when the floor was in place." He turned to Cynthia and wagged a finger at her. "Don't let anyone take you there after dark. It is far too easy to get lost. Thieves work unhindered in the shadowed maze."

Cynthia shivered at his ominous tone, and even Dora felt a twinge of fear.

Inga hurried to change the topic. "Can you tell us more about the animals they kept? I read somewhere they had lions. Is that true?"

The guide leapt at the question, launching into an explanation of the far reaches of the Roman empire. Stretching as far north as modern-day England, and south into Africa, the ancient people encountered many strange creatures.

Cynthia looked back into the centre of the arena. "It must have been huge to the men and women sent there to fight. But for a lion? There isn't room enough to outrun one."

"No, indeed. However, I always felt there were others who had it worse," the guide said. He explained, "There was an ancient prison in the forum, not too far from here. Imagine being consigned to a cell there, and hearing the lions roar night after night. You'd never sleep for fear of when it would be your turn to face the beasts."

Dora glanced at Cynthia, worried about how the dark tale would affect her. She needn't have been concerned. Cynthia turned to the guide, her eyes once again wide with excitement. "Can we go there next? To the forum, I mean?"

The man rattled off a price for the additional tour and Dora agreed. The sprawling forum ruins, lunch, and an afternoon gelato filled the remaining hours of the workday. By the time it was six in the evening, all three women were flagging.

"Come on, now," Dora cajoled. "One last stop and then we can put our feet up at home."

They returned to the address Mary had provided to her employer. This time, the street was much busier. Working men and women hurried their way along the pavement, ready to reach the comfort of their own homes.

Inga and Cynthia slowed their steps, falling behind the closer they got to the door. When Dora spun around to see what was holding them up, Inga made a proposal.

"Why don't Cynthia and I wait outside? There's no need for us to crowd the house."

Dora rolled her eyes. "Fine, but have a look around. See if anything catches your eye. I still want to know why Mary chose to live here. I doubt it was a simple as availability and rent. There are plenty of rooms for let in Rome."

Dora gritted her teeth and then knocked on the door. This time, a man answered. He had a friendly face and bore traces of icing sugar on his cheek. Before he could say hello, the little girl came flying along the corridor, shouting for his attention.

"One moment," he said in an apologetic tone.

Dora glanced to her left and noted that Inga and Cynthia were hurrying away.

"Mi scusi," the man said, catching Dora's attention again.

The little girl was standing beside him, doing her best impersonation of an angel. Dora wasn't fooled for a second.

"My wife is cooking dinner, so it is my turn to play with the children. Are you Maria's friend? Here for the box?" He was well prepared, having already tied it with string. He handed

Dora the parcel. It was roughly the size of a hatbox. "Thank you for taking this task off our hands. My wife took the news hard."

Dora thanked him for keeping Mary's things and then let him get back to his role of dutiful father. The box wasn't so heavy that it required two hands to hold, but neither was it so light that Dora wanted to carry it for long. She searched the pavement to see where the others had gone.

Cynthia was the closest. She called her name and waved to get Cynthia's attention. Once she caught up, she asked, "Did Inga abandon you?"

"I stopped to window shop. She's further ahead. Up there. She's talking to someone."

At first, Dora didn't see her. Then she realised Inga was indeed busy talking to a man. A familiar man with a moustache, bushy beard, and scarring on his neck.

Dora grabbed Cynthia's arm and tugged her into a narrow alley between two buildings. She held a finger to her lips to keep Cynthia quiet.

Soon after, the man walked past. He was lost in thought and paid no mind to the women tucked in the alley.

Dora shoved the package into Cynthia's hands and whispered, "I've got to follow him. Go get Inga."

Dora hurried out, walking as quickly as she dared to keep up. The man never once glanced back. He waved hello to a clerk in the vegetable market and doffed his hat at a passing woman. Dora shadowed him when he turned the corner, but came to an abrupt stop when he went inside the entry to a block of flats.

Did this explain Mary's choice of neighbourhood?

Dora backtracked and quickly spotted her friends. They were both staring at her in confusion. As soon as Dora reached their sides, she asked Inga, "How did you know to stop him?"

Inga was equally dumbstruck by what had happened. "That man? I didn't stop him. He stopped me."

Dora's jaw dropped — a rare occurrence. She waved for Inga to explain.

"He introduced himself as Brandon Shaw. He recognised me — called me Sister Inga. Said I'd cared for him during the war. He thanked me. I'll admit it was strange, but not impossible. We cared for a fair few soldiers during our time at the front. I daresay most times, we were more memorable to them than the reverse."

"Maybe..." Dora thought back to the blue door that led into a block of flats. "But I don't like the coincidence."

Inga tapped Dora's arm to get her attention. "What coincidence? Who was he? You're speaking in a code no one else can understand."

Dora dragged her focus back to her friend. "That man is a clerk at the embassy. He's the one who issued Clark and Rex with their official documents."

Chapter 15
A Roman Gala

Rex was wrangling his bowtie into place when Dora returned from her day's activities. She threw open the door to their bedroom, slunk inside, and collapsed facedown on their bed.

"My feet are so sore, even the blisters have blisters," she moaned into the bedspread.

It took Rex a moment to make sense of her muffled words. He hurried to her side, picked up a foot, and began massaging it, taking care to avoid the red marks from her shoes. "I've got good news and bad news. The good is that you've got time for a short soak in the bathtub before we have to leave."

"Leave?" Dora jerked her head up from the bed and finally took a good look at Rex. "Oh no. The society event. I completely forgot."

"Yes, that was the bad news. I figured as much when you didn't turn up an hour ago. But there's no need to stress. Nonna Matilda is arranging for someone to style your hair. Your dress is hanging in the dressing room, and the bathroom is all yours."

Dora hoisted herself off the bed and dragged herself to the bathroom. She squealed in delight a moment later.

"Found the glass of wine and plate of nibbles, I take it?" Rex called out.

Dora came back into the bedroom, wearing nothing more than a bath sheet. She kissed him on the lips. "Thank you for taking such good care of me, darling."

"Consider this me upholding my vows. Now scoot. You're wasting your limited relaxing time."

Dora gave him a last peck on the lips. "Time spent with you is never wasted. Even if my sore feet beg to disagree."

Rex left Dora to get ready and went downstairs to join Clark for a drink. The men took their cocktails out to the garden terrace.

"Do you have the list of people we need to interview?" Rex asked Clark.

"I've done better than that, old chap. I've got four." Clark rifled in his coat pocket and pulled out four small sheets of paper. "One each for you and me. You might as well take Dora's for safekeeping."

"And the last one?"

"It's for your grandmother. I figured you and I could chat up the friendly ladies, Theodora can question the men. For your grandmother, I left the grand dames of society who are least likely to succumb to our charms."

Interviewing the ambassador's butler and other house staff had required all his attention. He hadn't given a thought to prioritising the list of Ennio's clients. He patted Clark on the back and congratulated him on a job well done.

Clark raised a toast in his own honour and then added, "Rex, you aren't the only one capable of solving mysteries. I daresay that I've got a deft hand. You should rely upon me more often."

Rex nearly choked on his drink. If only he could tell Clark just how instrumental he'd been in each of Rex's investigations thus far! Rex was, however, sworn to secrecy. He'd never reveal his role as a spy without Lord Audley's express permission.

Yet, the seed rested there in his mind. Time would tell whether it would take root.

Dora arrived, dressed to the nines in a new gown and another one of her circular pendants. Rex spotted no sign of her earlier weariness until his gaze landed on her ankles. There, if one looked closely, he spied the edge of a sticking plaster rising above the back of her shoe.

On the car ride over, Rex passed Dora her list and explained the plan to her and Clark. "We'll have to take care of how we approach the conversations. We don't want word to get around that Ennio Pianoforti had a thief in their employ, especially if we're wrong on the matter. I suggest we approach the question from a few different angles — missing items, unreliable servants, etcetera."

The car deposited the trio outside the front entrance of the Grand Hotel de la Minerve. Located near the Pantheon and Parliament buildings, it had long played host to guests from the highest levels of society. This evening's event was in the Salone Olimpo.

Bernini's half-dozen marble statues were meant to be the main draw of the room. However, their pale white limbs faded into the background when compared to the sparkling gowns, black suits, and expensive jewels of the guests. Rex, Dora, and Clark strode into the room as a confident trio, but soon split to go their own way.

Rex spotted his grandmother holding court on the opposite side of the room and went to say hello. He kissed her cheeks, noting the healthy glow to her skin. "Good evening, Grandmama. You're looking particularly lovely this evening."

Edith basked in his compliment. "The Mediterranean clime

agrees with me. Warm air, plenty of sunshine, and your sister's youthful energy have given me a new lease on life."

"Excellent. I'm in need of a little assistance. Could you spare me a moment of your time?"

Rex led his grandmother to a quieter corner of the room. He retrieved her list from his pocket and handed it over. A quick word of explanation was all she needed.

She patted him on the hand. "Leave it with me, for now. Bring your lovely companion over for lunch tomorrow and I'll tell you what I learned."

Rex grabbed a glass of prosecco from a passing waiter and then wandered the floor until he spotted his first target.

Her ladyship was wealthy, bored, and on the hunt for her fourth husband. She'd been a beauty in her youth and age had hardly lessened her appeal. However, outliving three husbands had earned her a certain reputation. Rex layered on the charm. "Lady Golding, what a delight to find you here. I hadn't heard you were in Rome."

"I'm working my way back north after spending the winter in Greece," she explained. "Are you here alone?"

"Err, no. Not exactly. I arrived with Miss Laurent and Lord Clark. You're acquainted with Lord Clark, correct?" Rex watched as her smile widened. Poor Clark would string him up by his toes if he overheard Rex dangling him in front of her nose. In Rex's defence, he had said he wanted to take a more active role in the investigations.

Lady Golding, however, had no complaints about the quality of local help. She travelled with an entourage of trusted servants and never let anyone wander about her home. Rex continued his spin around the room, but had no better luck. Lady Collins's only complaint was about a housemaid who knocked over a priceless vase. Lady Sampson squashed the topic all together, turning the conversation into a discussion about the availability of her daughter.

It was one of the rare occasions when Rex wished he had a ring on his finger.

Still, he did his part to continue their search for clues by asking her daughter for a dance. Lady Felicia batted her lashes at him while he spun her around. She admitted to taking piano lessons, but was sorry to report her skills were minimal. "Mother refuses to accept my artistic limitations. She insisted on tuning the piano."

"Who came to do the work?" Rex asked, latching onto the potential lead.

Lady Felicia turned her face up to him and fluttered her lashes. "The tuner came before we arrived in Rome. I'd be happy to ask our butler for more information. You could pay me a call. Say tomorrow? In time for tea?"

Thankfully, the song ended in time to save Rex. He spotted Dora standing on the other side of the room and said he had to check on her. Lady Felicia took one look at Dora and abandoned the cause.

Rex could see Dora's face. She was playing her role to the hilt, flashing smiles and throwing her head back in a laugh. With the way the crowd was situated, Rex didn't have a view of her audience. He knew her well enough to recognise the signs. Whomever she was speaking with was not a genuine friend.

He caught her eye as he walked over, raising an eyebrow in a silent question. Her smile widened a fraction, shifting from performance art to genuine joy.

"Darling! There you are! I was just telling the others about our adventures around Europe." She held out a hand and encouraged Rex to join them.

A gap opened up in the circle and Rex finally saw the faces of the rest of the group. He didn't need any introduction. The man with the thick moustache covering his top lip was none other than the Italian king himself. Between the coin in Rex's pocket and the postage stamps gracing his mail, the stately profile of Re Vittorio Emanuele III was easily recognisable.

It was the other man who caused Rex to draw up short.

Mussolini. Italy's new Prime Minister.

Mussolini's balding head gleamed under the light of the Murano chandeliers. His piercing eyes scanned Rex from head to toe, taking his full measure at a glance. His expression never changed, and yet, somehow Rex felt he'd been found wanting.

This was the man they'd been sent to understand. From what they'd heard, he was seen as much as a violent brute as a saviour for the working class man. His rise to power hadn't been bloodless. And yet, there in the opulent hotel ballroom, surrounded by wealth and power, Mussolini was completely at ease.

Rex couldn't say the same for the people around him. Everyone, Dora included, seemed keen to keep him happy. Even the king himself took care not to upstage Mussolini.

Rex understood then why Lord Audley relied so much on insights from his agents in the field. Seeing Mussolini in his home environment, noticing the expressions on people's faces and the deference in their tone, was invaluable. This was not something that could be learned by inviting a leader for a state visit or at a meeting on the world stage.

England would be wise to keep a close eye on this man. He was not going to relinquish his hold on Italy without a fight. Rex doubted that anyone there would dare to take him on.

But now wasn't the time for further intelligence gathering. Resolving the question of the ambassador's guilt or innocence was their top priority.

And so Rex widened his own smile and nodded a greeting

to their hosts. "Piacere, piacere," he said, taking great care to correctly pronounce the Italian greeting.

"Mussolini was telling us the most delightful story about his daughter Edda," Dora explained.

"Delightful for you, perhaps, given you are also a headstrong woman. While I am proud of her spirit, I pity the man who tries to tame her," Mussolini replied.

"Tame who?" a man's voice asked. The crowd parted, allowing Sir Francis to join the group.

Rex tensed at the ambassador's unexpected appearance. Wasn't the man supposed to be in hiding out of fear of being arrested?

"Francesco! I feared you wouldn't accept my invitation." King Vittorio held out a hand to Sir Francis.

The ambassador executed a perfect bow over the king's hand, showing the man the deference due, and then righted himself. He glanced over his shoulder and then motioned for someone else to hurry. "Re Vittorio, I must introduce you to Miss Adams, a relative of my wife. She is staying with us for a time."

Prudence stepped forward, taking her place beside the ambassador. She bobbed a curtsy to the king and the prime minister. "It is an honour," she said in a quiet voice.

The king beamed at her. Mussolini paid her no mind other than a curt acknowledgment. An untitled woman, whose only relation was under suspicion of murder, hardly warranted his interest.

The men resumed their conversation, with Dora flattering them in turns. She had a way of doing so that Rex envied. Her words were never hollow, her tone never forced. Somehow, she made everyone with whom she spoke feel special.

Rex was superfluous at that moment. He prepared to excuse himself when Prudence caught his eye. She had stepped into Sir

Francis's shadow, not leaving his side, but nonetheless, also not one of the group. She'd certainly mastered the role of the subservient, docile female relative.

After all the time Rex had spent with Dora and Inga, he had little doubt that Prudence was likely intelligent. Here, in a foreign land, with no escape, she must be incredibly isolated.

Rex didn't give himself time to second-guess his thoughts. He murmured an excuse and left Dora's side, circling around the small enclave until he arrived at Prudence.

"If you're not too busy, there is someone I'd like you to meet."

Prudence glanced around the room of strangers, sizing up the guests. "Someone you know?"

Rex flashed her a toothy grin. "Someone I know exceptionally well. And whom I'm certain would be delighted to hear you're in town. Just today, she was lamenting the shortage of dinner guests capable of carrying on an intelligent conversation."

His subtle flattery and recognition of her skills did the trick. Prudence accepted Rex's outstretched hand.

Rex guided her across the room, aiming for a silver-haired woman in an empire-waist, royal blue gown. "Grandmama," he called as they approached. "Have you said hello to Miss Adams? I'm sure you agree we must have her over for dinner."

Chapter 16
The Flat Swap

The party and accompanying supper lasted until the wee hours of the night. By mutual agreement, everyone had a lie-in the following morning before regrouping for lunch at the home of Rex's grandmother. Over a light meal, Dora, Rex, Clark, and Edith exchanged thoughts about what they'd learned at the party.

"Did anyone find any evidence of theft? Any hints of dissatisfaction or concern about Mary's visits to tune the pianos?" Dora asked.

"Not a word," Edith answered. "I heard plenty of complaints about Italy, most centring on the fact that it is not England. But as for our victim, her visits had barely registered."

"Same for me," Clark agreed. "And after the indignities I suffered! Two married women offered indecent proposals, and a third attempted to arrange an engagement with her daughter."

Dora failed to bite back a laugh, earning a glower from Clark. "My apologies, Clark. I can't imagine why anyone would think you open to such propositions."

Rex raised a hand. "I can..."

Clark lobbed his napkin in Rex's direction. "E tu, Brute?

I've been on my best behaviour since we left England. You should at least acknowledge I've turned over a new leaf."

"You absolutely have," Edith agreed. "Enough on that topic. Let's move to the drawing room, where we can all be more comfortable. I'm keen to hear what you all thought of King Vittorio and Prime Minister Mussolini. "

They settled into the drawing room, Dora and Rex on the sofa, while Clark and Edith availed themselves of a pair of wingback chairs. Bright sun flooded the room through the tall windows. Between the creamy yellow paint on the walls, the mosaic tile floor, and the red and orange rugs, the room immediately lifted everyone's spirits.

"I must confess, I didn't speak with either of the men," Clark said. "I was too busy fighting off women."

"What a tough life you lead, my friend. What of you, Grandmama?" Rex glanced at Edith. "You've more experience than anyone of us at mingling with men in power."

"I'm not sure about that. Our Theodora has done her fair share of circulating around the world stage. Nonetheless, I'll offer my opinion. I'm interested to see whether Theodora agrees." Edith settled more comfortably in her chair. "Unlike our King George, Vittorio Emanuele didn't receive the same training for eventually taking the throne. Even now, after over two decades in power, he still looks to ride someone else's coattails rather than take the helm himself. That was clear in the way he deferred to Mussolini throughout the evening."

"I first met the king three years ago," Dora said. "The man revels in his status, but has little interest in his responsibilities to the people he guides. It is likely why he and Sir Francis became friends. They are two of a kind."

"They are, indeed. I assume you all noticed at supper that while Mussolini sat on the king's right, Sir Francis was there on his left." Edith turned to Dora. "I didn't get the chance to speak with Mussolini. You did, however."

"The world is right to monitor him. He's somewhat terrifying in his determination and sheer brute strength. But that isn't as relevant now as the way he acted toward Sir Francis, nor the things he said about England."

Clark and Rex both sat up straighter.

Dora continued, "Mussolini's gaze is ever calculating. To him, we're nothing more than pieces on a game board. Toward Sir Francis, he displayed the polite interest one expects for the ambassador of an ally. It would have been so easy for Mussolini to have cut him out of conversations and otherwise express his silent displeasure. Yet, I saw nothing of the sort."

"What about when he spoke?" Edith asked, equally intrigued as her grandson. "What did he say about England? Did he make any references that led you to believe he wanted something from Sir Francis?"

"Mussolini made a point of saying that England would come to respect Italy. It's no secret that he feels the country got a raw deal at the end of the Great War. He said he depended upon Sir Francis and everyone else in attendance to tell the British government that Italy is changing. He promised he'd bring stability to the nation's government, and drive economic growth." Dora crossed her arms and shook her head. "It doesn't make sense that he'd be behind the accusation against Sir Francis. What would he have to gain from threatening Italy's relationship with England? If anything, I walked away understanding why he's giving Sir Francis time to clear his name. That would make for a much simpler solution for everyone."

"Where does that leave you?" Edith asked.

"I've been asking myself that question since I woke up. Despite being on international shores, this smacks of a domestic incident. We have a British woman dead, and a British man accused. The murder happened outside the ambassador's home. I still think the killer came from inside. But I'm not sure whether it was a member of the ambassador's household, or someone else related to the embassy."

"It's a riddle, indeed. On that note, I'll leave you to it. I promised to accompany Inga on another outing."

Clark turned to Dora and Rex. "What about us? What's next on our investigation list?"

Dora feigned a heavy sigh. "Boring work, I'm afraid. I've asked the embassy to send over the personnel files on everyone employed at the ambassador's residence, and any staff members who regularly visit."

As expected, Clark's shoulders dropped. "I suppose I could lend a hand with that...if there's nothing else."

Dora looked up at the ceiling, pretending to consider his question. "If you don't mind taking a walk, it might be a good idea to visit the telegraph office to ask if Lord Audley has sent a reply. After that, why not rub shoulders with those journalists again? Maybe ask them when they got here."

Clark leapt to his feet. "You can count on me. Shall I meet you here later?"

"We'll need to change before dinner. Why don't we meet at home at half seven or eight? We can ride over together."

Clark thanked Dora again and hurried out the drawing-room door before she had second thoughts.

When they were finally alone in the room, Rex turned to his wife. "What's this about personnel files? And why, pray tell, did you say we'd go through them on our own?"

Dora told Rex about her visit to Mary's address. "We went back later to collect the box of personal items. As feared, there was nothing in there of value. However, I spotted Brandon Shaw passing on the pavement. I followed him and discovered he lives around the corner. Since we were due to dine here, I sent off the message this morning requesting he bring the files round."

"So we're not pawing through paperwork?"

"Unless you disagree, I'd like to hear what he knew about our victim. If he claims ignorance, we'll have to go through the files to learn who else resides at the boarding house."

"That's a reasonable plan." Rex rose to stretch his legs. "Like you, I can't believe it is a coincidence that Mary lived so close to one of the embassy staff. If Brandon's daily route took him past her front door, surely they must have crossed paths."

"Until we know more, we need Brandon to view us as allies. We must tread carefully."

Mr Shaw arrived half an hour later and the dowager's butler escorted him into the drawing room. The poor man was so nervous that the stack of files in his hands trembled. "Lord Reginald, I brought the files you requested."

Rex leapt to his feet and hurried over to him. "My goodness, those look heavy. Let me help you."

While Rex set the files on a nearby table, Dora invited Brandon to have a seat. "You look positively parched. Shall I ring for your English tea? No, wait. It is too hot for such a drink. I'll ask them to bring a pitcher of limonata."

Her warm welcome and steady patter put the man at ease. A rap on the door signalled the arrival of the butler with the requested tray of drinks. He poured the sparkling drink into tall glasses garnished with a slice of lemon, and then left them to continue their discussions.

Rex cleared his throat. "Since you're here, Brandon, perhaps you can save us from searching through all those files."

"I can't promise to know anything, but I'm willing to give it a go."

"Excellent. I wondered where the embassy staff live. I must

admit, I have little experience with such matters. Is there a dormitory? Does the embassy rent flats on your behalf?"

Brandon took a sip of his drink before replying. "That depends on whether the staff member has a family. Those with a wife and children arrange their own accommodation."

"And the others?" Dora asked.

"There are two options. For those of us in roles with longer working hours, there is a boarding house near the Colosseum. Employees with more regular working hours stay in another building on the outskirts." Brandon gave a wry smile. "I must admit that those particular arrangements never made much sense to me. The people with the most time to enjoy the city are those who live far away from the sights."

Rex chuckled politely. "What about you?"

"I'm at the beck and call of the ambassador and his private secretary. I live in town. Do you want me to separate the personnel files based on where people live?"

"That would be useful. Let's start with those in the centre."

Brandon gathered the files into his lap and sorted through them. He passed a stack of around ten over. Rex flipped through them, angling them so Dora also had a view.

Dora latched onto Rex's hand when she saw the title of private secretary next to the names of one of the men. She recalled the building front that Brandon had entered the day before, but this time repainted the door from blue to red.

She'd seen that building before. Three years before, to be exact. But another man had been in the role of private secretary.

Dora moved her hand off of Rex's arm. She pointed to the job title and prayed he'd understand her hint.

Rex closed the file and opened the next. It was Brandon's. "It says here you moved into the centre three years ago. The other day, you mentioned you'd been here since the end of the war. Where did you live when you first arrived?"

"I was a lowly clerk, my lord. I didn't move into the centre until I was promoted into the ambassador's office." Cool as ice, Brandon lifted his glass of lemonade.

A shape formed in Dora's mind. She cocked her head to the side and feigned confusion. "I was here then. Sir Francis was very upset. He'd had some difficulty with his private secretary. Am I remembering that correctly?"

Brandon froze for a split second with his glass halfway to his mouth. If Dora hadn't been focusing on him so intently, she'd have missed it.

"Yes, it was a terrible tragedy. The man died, err, unexpectedly, let's say."

"So the man listed here, a Mr Gibbs, he arrived then?"

"No. Mr Gibbs was in my role. Sir Francis promoted him to private secretary, and I moved into the clerk's position."

Rex returned to the file that had originally caught Dora's attention. He skimmed a finger down the page until he came to the address section. "Mr Gibbs was already living in the centre. How does that work? Did he move to a nicer flat, and you took his? That seems like a lot of faff."

Brandon shifted in his chair. "The flats are all the same. Mr Gibbs stayed in his, and I took over the vacancy. It wasn't so much a faff as awkward. I was tasked with packing the previous tenant's things and shipping them to his family in England."

"That must have been difficult." Rex cast a sideways glance at Dora, but she remained silent. "Let's go through the second stack now."

Dora only half paid attention while Rex and Brandon finished their task. She was busy filling in the picture in her head.

Three years ago, the ambassador's private secretary had sold state secrets, and killed himself to avoid prosecution. Now

Brandon Shaw lived in his flat. Had Brandon taken over more than just his lease?

Was that why Mary was in the neighbourhood? Had she been working with Brandon? Or did the poor girl stumble across his secret? A picture formed in her mind's eye, and it wasn't pretty.

If the embassy had another traitor in its midst, this time she was going to catch him red-handed.

Chapter 17
A Dinner Party

R ex poured himself a drink while he waited for Dora to finish getting ready. She rarely took so long to get dressed for dinner at his grandmother's. Tonight, however, she was far too distracted by their investigation to think about clothing and hair. Rex feared that if he abandoned the room, she'd end up sitting on the bed, scribbling notes.

Dora sat at her dressing table, staring at his face in the mirror instead of hers. "I'm telling you, Rex, Brandon Shaw knows too much. I didn't buy his explanation for how he ended up renting the flat. I bet he was there to make sure more evidence of the secretary's criminal acts didn't come to light. Then he took over the lease and the government spying."

"Perhaps, but there's an awfully long gap here between the crimes. Do you honestly believe Brandon Shaw, or anyone for that matter, could get away with selling state secrets for three years?" He waved at her hand. "Powder your nose, darling. We're running behind."

Dora patted the puff against her nose, forehead, and chin, all the while frowning at her reflection. "What if Brandon laid low for a time? In his shoes, that's exactly what I'd do."

Rex set his glass aside and approached his wife. He took the powder puff from her hand and laid it on the dressing table. "You are like a dog with a bone once you get a suspect in your sights. However, I must ask you to pause that line of thought until tomorrow morning."

Dora sighed. "You're right, of course. I'm sorry. We're on the cusp of a solution to this riddle, and my mind refuses to let go."

"Don't abandon all hope. We might learn something interesting from Prudence. We can ask her if Sir Francis spoke with any of the journalists," Rex reminded her. He picked up a tube of lipstick and passed it to her. "Swipe some of this on so we can go. I promise, first thing tomorrow, I'll give you, Brandon Shaw, and our murder case my full attention."

As always, the Dowager Duchess was resplendent. She wore a simpler gown and gold jewellery, setting the tone for a quieter evening in with close friends and family. Caledonia stood at her side, smiling in welcome at their guests. Both women embraced Dora and allowed Rex and Clark to kiss their cheeks.

"Did you forget Inga and Harris?" Edith asked, looking past them at the front door.

"They decided it was too nice an evening to be in the car, so they are walking over," Rex answered.

Clark leaned close to Dora and wiggled his eyebrows. "I suspect the two lovebirds simply wanted a few minutes to themselves."

Rex had to give his grandmother credit. She needed little direction to take their mixed group in hand. She directed each of them to an empty chair and told them to make themselves at home. When Inga and Harris arrived, she slotted them into the empty seats. Despite being much younger than the others, Caledonia chatted happily.

Then the guest of honour arrived. Sheffield, upright as

always in his starched white shirt and black tails, announced Miss Prudence Adams before letting her into the room.

Edith rose from her chair and hurried over to welcome Prudence into her home. "What a lovely dress, Prudence. That shade of peach brings out the rose tones in your complexion."

Prudence blushed under the compliment. "You're too kind, your grace. I've had this dress for some time."

"No sense in replacing something so flattering. That's my rule of thumb as well. And please, call me Edith. We don't stand on ceremony here." Edith carried on with the introductions. "My grandchildren, Rex and Caledonia. You've met Theodora and Clark. Over there are Inga and Harris. They are dear friends of Theodora who have earned a place in my heart as well. Now please, sit down. Sheffield, can you get Prudence a drink?"

Prudence took the empty seat on the sofa next to Caledonia. The two women sat across from Rex and Dora, giving Rex a prime view of their guest. He studied her carefully, making use of his spy training.

Prudence murmured a quiet hello to Caledonia and nodded at the rest. She sank back into the sofa cushions as though attempting to disappear. This was why he knew so little about her personality, despite having crossed paths with her in the past. She preferred to fade into the background rather than speak up.

He took care not to stare at her, lest he attract her attention, but he flicked a glance her way every chance that he got. The first two times, she had her gaze on the floor or directed at the glass in her hands. He watched a moment longer and caught her using his trick. When attention was elsewhere, she raised her eyes and studied the others, one by one.

Perhaps Dora was right. There was more to Prudence than

met the eye. He was suddenly much more interested in finding out whether her still waters ran deep.

At a lull in the conversation, Rex's grandmother called Prudence's name. "How are you finding Rome? Is this your first trip?"

"It is," Prudence replied. "I'd hoped to get the chance to explore, but now is hardly the time to ask anything of Sir Francis. You all must have been here many times. Surely you have more interesting tales to recount."

"I bet Theodora does," Caledonia piped up. "Tell us something from your previous visit."

"Is that when you first met Sir Francis?" Prudence asked. "Given your propensity for adventures, I'm sure the story is a doozy."

Rex carefully composed his face so as not to hint just how much of an adventure that trip had been. He had to give it to Dora. With Inga pitching in, she painted a picture of a typical tourist visit punctuated by upper crust events.

None too soon, Sheffield announced dinner, and they all filed into the dining room. Once again, his grandmother had taken control over the seating plan. She sat Prudence between Dora and Caledonia, with Inga across the table. Clark sat on Inga's left, and Harris on her right next to Edith. Rex took the chair at the foot of the table, playing co-host to his grandmother.

Over appetisers and the main course, Dora and Inga coaxed Prudence from her shell. They started, of course, with books. Dora took advantage of a lull in the conversation to toss out the opening volley. "Have you any interest in crime fiction, Prudence?"

"I've read most of the Sherlock Holmes series. Why do you ask?"

"Have you read anything by Agatha Christie? She's a newer author, but I must say that I am quite enjoying reading about a sleuth set in the present day. In her books, there is no crime too difficult for Hercule Poirot to solve."

"We could certainly use his help now with Sir Francis." Prudence sighed. "It is a predicament. I still cannot fathom how he ended up cast in the role of killer."

"Indeed," Dora agreed. "And to think, the poor young woman was in both Edith's home and yours prior to her death."

"Tuning the piano," Caledonia hastened to add. "She did an excellent job."

"Here, yes... but at the ambassador's residence, the butler told Rex he found the woman wandering about the house!"

"He did?" Caledonia gasped and turned to Prudence. "Did you see her?"

Prudence shook her head. "I'm surprised Jenkins noticed, given how many people there are coming and going at any time. Sir Francis is often closeted in meetings. More than once, I've bumped into a member of the embassy staff looking for the toilet or asking for a telephone. The piano tuner likely had a perfectly good reason, but Jenkins refused to listen. He didn't hide his disapproval of a woman doing what he perceived to be a man's job."

Rex believed that well enough, but he was more interested in the first part of Prudence's statement. He shifted in his seat so he could see around the centrepiece. "What about that day? You mentioned that Sir Francis had worked from the residence. Did you happen to run into any of his staff?"

Prudence took a moment to consider the question before answering. "Maybe? To be honest, at the time, I wasn't aware the day was going to be significant. It has run together with the others. You should ask Sir Francis's secretary or his clerk. One of them will know."

Rex felt the hairs on his arms rise. "They were both there? The secretary and the clerk?"

"They are always there. Them, the deputy heads, the event planners, guards, visiting dignitaries. The list is miles long, I'm afraid. Pity your Mrs Christie isn't here. Hercule Poirot would no doubt find some hidden clue that reveals all."

Inga intervened. "That isn't how Poirot solves crimes. He is a master of human nature and psychology. He notes the quirks and unsaid things, puts them together with the evidence, and ultimately determines who is a secret killer. Even in a house as busy as the one in which you live would pose little challenge. He'd weed through the suspects, narrowing ever down, until only one remained. That is what Clark and Rex are attempting to do."

"Far too slowly, and much more modestly," Clark said, piping up for once.

Prudence sniffed at Clark's comment. "Harder than it seems in the crime novels? I must say, I was surprised when Sir Francis said he'd reached out to Lord Rex for help. I wasn't aware you had any training in police matters."

"I don't," Rex admitted freely. None of the mysteries he'd solved had been crimes he could pass over to the police.

"And yet, your grandmother recommended you to Sir Francis." Prudence's eyes slid over to Edith's face. "Sir Francis was so relieved after you spoke with him. It was the part about Rex helping Prince Albert with some trouble he had. What was that?"

Prudence was entirely focused on Edith's face. As a result, she completely missed seeing Clark stiffen. Rex slid his foot forward, taking care to not rustle the tablecloth, and pressed it down onto Clark's left foot.

To her credit, Edith showed no signs of being under pressure. She lifted her glass and took a sip of her wine, making Prudence wait while she savoured the robust Chianti. "It was boys being boys... before the wedding. Nothing nearly as serious as this case, but I knew Sir Francis would feel most relieved to hear Rex is accustomed to helping those in power. You know, Sir Francis is in line for the throne."

Prudence flattened her lips. "Yes, he's mentioned it a time or two."

Edith leaned forward and lowered her voice. "Please, don't let this get back to Sir Francis, but Rex and Clark are filling in until proper help can arrive. Lord Audley has dispatched someone from the Foreign Office. As soon as they arrive, my grandson will hand everything over."

"Really?" Prudence gasped. She turned to face the other end of the table.

"I've been updating him via telegram," Clark said, without missing a beat.

"And thank goodness for that," Dora chimed in. "While it has been fun pretending to be Poirot, I'm looking forward to returning to our itinerary. Pompeii will be absolutely dreadful if the temperatures continue to rise."

"But Capri will be a delight, especially if you wear the new bathing costume you purchased," Rex added with a wink.

From there, Inga picked up the conversation, turning the talk away from the investigation and on to less explosive topics. It was likely the first time in history that Pompeii was considered safer ground.

Rex kept waiting for Prudence to ask another question, or twist the conversation back to current matters. But it was as though she read his mind. For the remainder of the night, she was a perfectly behaved guest, speaking up when asked, and ceding the floor when others knew more.

Perhaps it was the wine and bitters, but by the end of the evening, Rex's suspicions had faded away.

He recalled the words of his upper school tutor. The man

had repeated a quote by Edmund Burke so often, Rex could still recite it from memory.

'The first and simplest emotion which we discover in the human mind, is curiosity.'

Prudence had ventured to Rome with the best of intentions. It was hardly her fault she was caught in the middle of a troublesome situation. In her shoes, Rex's curiosity and concern would be never ending. He could hardly blame her for doing the same.

Chapter 18
The Cleaning Crew

By the time the evening ended, Dora was confident that there was something more to Prudence. Her questions had been too pointed for someone who didn't have a reputation for gossip. Yet, she'd dared to go toe-to-toe with the Dowager Duchess of Rockingham. Rex and Clark thought little of her, but Dora suspected those supposed still waters hid a depth of intrigue.

Edith obviously felt the same. When her guests declared it past time for them to go, she proposed they meet again the next day. She invited Clark and Prudence to join her and Caledonia for a tour of the Vatican museum. She refused to take no for an answer, and Caledonia lent her own words of encouragement to the cause. Prudence eventually gave in, and firmly cornered, Clark quickly followed suit.

Clark spent the walk home peppering Dora with questions about art and architecture. "With those three intelligent women running circles around me, I'll look a right fool if I don't have anything to add to the conversation. Since neither you nor Rex offered to keep me company tomorrow, I expect you to lend a hand tonight."

On any other evening, Dora would have been happy to help. But that night, she had other things weighing on her mind. She slowed her step and glanced over her shoulder to where Inga was walking behind her. "You found some local guidebooks in the study, didn't you? Could you point Clark in the right direction?"

Inga understood immediately. "Of course. I know exactly the ones you mean."

When they reached Nonna Matilda's home, Inga took Clark by the arm and led him toward the study. That left Dora free to hurry upstairs with Rex in hot pursuit.

Dora rushed into the bedroom. She kicked off her shoes and then studied the chairs in the room. Too short. Too unstable.

Rex was hovering just inside the doorway. "Care to clue me in?"

"In a minute. First, can you go to Inga's and Harris's room and borrow their desk chair?"

Rex swallowed his questions and bustled off to complete his assignment. Meanwhile, Dora disappeared into her dressing room. She dragged her travelling case out of the corner and shifted clothes on the rack. By the time Rex arrived with the chair, she'd cleared the floor space.

"Where do you want this?"

"Over here. Don't run off. I need you to make sure I don't fall."

Rex latched onto the back of the chair. "I'm not going anywhere until you explain what you're doing."

Dora used Rex's shoulder for support as she climbed onto the chair. She reached up and pushed on the ceiling. To the casual observer, the floral motif and trails of leafy vines seemed extravagant. In truth, they disguised the entrance to the attic. If you didn't know exactly where to push, you'd never get in.

Dora located the latch after a moment of searching. The

trap door dropped by an inch. Dora slid her hand around the edge until she found the piece of string that kept it from swinging all the way open. Seconds later, she guided the door open.

Attached to the other side of the door was a short, foldable ladder. Dora hopped off the chair, moved it aside, unfolded the metal rails, and invited Rex to follow her.

Wooden joists lined the low ceiling. Even though it was not tall, this section of the attic was utilised effectively. The storage area was meticulously organised. Rows of shelves held labelled wooden boxes. Dora chose the centre aisle and scanned them as she walked. She pulled out the one bearing her and Inga's initials. Inside lay a wrapped bundle.

"Carry this down for me, please. I need to put things back to rights."

Rex took the proffered bundle and preceded Dora down the ladder. Once they were again in the dressing room, she repeated the process in reverse until the room was back the way it had been.

Only then did she unwrap the bundle to reveal its contents. Two cotton dresses, made of sturdy fabric and smelling heavily of cleaning products, sat neatly folded inside. She picked them up and shook them out, wrinkling her nose against the harsh scent. "Not my favourite disguise," she murmured, "but I can't deny its effectiveness."

"Disguise for what?" Rex asked, his voice sharp as he lost the battle with his temper.

"I want the notes from the ambassador's meeting on the day Mary visited his house."

"We can ask Brandon Shaw to bring them round tomorrow."

"He's the one I'm investigating!" Dora swung around to face Rex. "What if Mary was wandering in search of

Brandon? She could have passed him something, or vice versa."

Rex scrunched his brow. "I don't know, Dora. How could they have planned such a thing in advance?"

Dora tapped him on the nose. "I won't know that until I've searched his files. Inga and I can use our old cleaning crew identities to get inside. The last crew goes in at midnight. If we hurry we can still make it."

"What do you need me to do?"

"Distract Clark. Talk to him about art, settle his nerves, remind him of his natural charm — whatever it takes to keep him occupied in the front of the house while we sneak out the back."

Rex gave Dora a salute and marched off to execute his orders. A sharp rap on the door signalled Inga's arrival. Although she grumbled about the late hour, there was no real heat in her words. They made quick work of wiping the flattering make-up from their faces and replacing it with powders, paints, and carefully drawn lines to make them look more haggard. With their wigs and dresses on and shoulders slumped, they were close enough to pass muster.

Nonna Matilda herself ferried them to the side entrance of the British embassy. A line of cleaners stood outside the door, waiting for the guard to let them in. The old woman proceeded them out of the car and walked directly toward the woman in charge. Nonna Matilda had a quiet word and then slipped a roll of bills into the hands of the leader of the cleaning team.

After she departed, the middle-aged woman rattled off a series of instructions to the other women. Two women stepped out of the line. She gave them money, and they left with smiles on their faces. The remaining cleaners shifted around to allow Dora and Inga to step into the queue. When the guard opened the door, he waved them all inside without a second glance.

The leader pointed the group in various directions, listing off their assignments. She sent Dora and Inga to the top floor, where the ambassador's office was located.

When they were alone, Inga whispered to Dora, "I thought Audley made it more difficult for people to sneak into the embassy. That guard didn't even check our names."

"He did, but he left a loophole that only Nonna Matilda can exploit. Case in point, you never know when he'll need someone to gain access while undercover."

Dora and Inga had used this particular disguise enough times to require no further conversations. The key to a successful execution was in doing both the fake job and the real one. They split up, one collecting rubbish from the bins, while the other swept the floor. They worked their way along the corridor. Once, a guard passed. He hummed under his breath, a catchy tune Dora didn't recognise, and nodded at them as he went by.

After almost an hour of cleaning, the pair reached the door marked with the ambassador's name. The handle turned smoothly. Dora flicked on the lights.

The room was just as Dora remembered. She was standing in a graciously appointed antechamber. Thick carpet in a blue and white stripe covered the floor. Wooden panelling covered the bottom half of the walls, with a chair rail separating it from the silk wallpaper. Expensive art from renowned British artists graced the walls.

This was the private secretary's domain. From his desk, he could both keep watch over visitors and be at the ambassador's beck and call. He kept his desk neat and had minimal personal items on it. When seated, the secretary's view was of the line of chairs set against the far wall.

Dora motioned for Inga to check the drawers of the secretary's desk. She instead opted for the doorway into a small alcove tucked in the side of the room. There, she found three metal filing cabinets and a metal desk with a typewriter on top. Brandon's name was etched into the nameplate.

She went through the files first. As expected, the man was well-organised. Each drawer revealed a tidy row of files, grouped by subject and labelled by date. The second filing cabinet proved to be the one with the meeting minutes. Dora tabbed through until she found the folder marked with the date in question. She filched the papers from inside, folded them up, and tucked them into her dress.

She hurried through the remaining cabinet drawers, but found nothing else unusual. She didn't have the time to search each folder, one by one. If needed, she could return the next night.

She gave the desk a last glance before turning away. A blue glass paperweight caught her eye. She'd seen it before. Here? She searched her prodigious memory for any hint of where she'd come across it. The juxtaposition of the fine glass and the simple metal desk was jarring.

She reached over, lifted it from atop a stack of papers, and carried into the light of the next room. The overhead lights revealed the dark splotch in the middle to be a pressed rose. A pressed English rose, to be precise.

"Psst," she whispered to Inga.

Inga glanced up from where she'd been tucking a stack of papers into her dress. "I found a week's worth of telegrams in the rubbish. He must have been carrying them around. I thought they might be useful. What are you holding?"

Dora offered Inga the paperweight. "Where have we seen this before?"

Inga scrutinised the object, her eyes narrowing as she searched her memory. Without a word, she spun around, placed it on the corner of the private secretary's desk, and stepped back.

"Yes, that's exactly where it sat three years ago. Now Brandon keeps it in his office. Any guesses why?"

Inga plucked the weight and passed it back to Dora. "None of them bode well. Is that all you found?"

"No, I also got the meeting minutes I wanted. Let's finish up and get out of here." Dora returned the paperweight to where she'd found it.

While Inga took care of searching through the remaining rubbish, Dora entered the ambassador's office. The spacious room had windows on two sides. Although there was a magnificent Georgian desk sitting at one end, the room lacked any other elements of a typical office. Sir Francis wasn't the type to want information at his fingertips. It was enough that his secretary and clerk brought him everything at a moment's notice.

Still, Dora scanned the room, looking for anything unusual or out of place. For the most part, it was exactly as she recalled. The only new addition was a photo of Sir Francis and his wife standing with King George and Queen Mary. Based on their clothing, Dora suspected it was from the recent royal wedding.

It was a reminder of what Sir Francis held most dear. His connection to the royal family, no matter how tenuous, was highly valued.

Dora couldn't come up with a single reason Sir Francis would have been outside the residence grounds on the night of the murder. But as for Mr Shaw, there was plenty to raise eyebrows.

Dora pulled a rag from where she'd tucked into her belt. She polished the frame, dusted the desk, and skipped past the empty bin. Methodically, she wiped away all traces of her presence.

Together, the women traipsed down the stairs, arms filled

with cleaning supplies. They deposited them with the rest and left with the other cleaners. Although they were in the clear, they didn't drop their personas until they arrived home.

Nonna Matilda's house was dark, the drapes all closed and lights out. Dora used the key the woman had provided to enter through the rear door. The clock on the wall said it was nearly three in the morning.

Although Dora was desperate to study the papers she'd taken, she recognised that doing so now would be a mistake. Already, the weight of sleep draped across her shoulders and slowed her motions. She wanted out of her clothes and back into her life.

"Regroup tomorrow? After breakfast?" Inga asked, as though she'd read Dora's mind.

"As soon as Clark is out the door. Then we can decide what to do next."

Chapter 19
Flat 1C

Rex let Dora sleep in until it was almost time for Clark to leave. She dressed in a hurry and made it downstairs to wish Clark luck before he went out the door.

After the door shut, she turned to Rex. "Is Inga awake yet?"

"Harris took a tray to their room," he answered. "You've got half an hour to eat and make yourself presentable before we're to meet in the library to review those papers you brought home."

Rex didn't need to tell Dora twice. She loaded her plate with fresh fruit and balanced it out with an extra-large, sugar-dusted apricot croissant. She washed it down with a cappuccino and then disappeared upstairs to finish getting ready.

At eleven on the dot, she was in the library, sitting with her feet up on a sofa in full view of the door. She arched a single eyebrow when they strode in. "Nice of you to show up."

Inga pulled up short. "That's an awfully confident remark from a woman wearing two different shoes."

Rex's eyes went straight to Dora's feet, just as Inga had intended. Of course, she was correct. Although the shoes were identical, one was black and the other dark blue.

Dora took her mishap on the chin and laughed with the rest

of them. Peace restored, she picked up the papers from the table and unfolded them. The stack was thicker than Rex had expected.

"These are all from one meeting? How long was it?" he asked.

Dora split the stack into two piles. "The number of pages is deceptive. I took both the handwritten notes, and the final typed minutes."

By mutual agreement, they began with the typed minutes. Harris retrieved his notepad and added the names of the attendees. It was a day-long session, with people popping in and out depending on the topic.

"Do we know what time Mary visited the residence?" Inga asked.

Rex checked the files they'd received from Pianoforti Ennio. "It says here the appointment was for ten in the morning. The butler told us that the job ran past an hour, and then he found her wandering around the house. Being generous, I'd say we're looking at a window of two hours, at the maximum."

Harris crossed off everyone from the afternoon session. The team leafed through the notes from the morning session, keeping a closer eye on the start and stop times for each meeting, along with the comings and goings of the staff. Rex noticed a discrepancy. He reached for the handwritten notes to double-check his suspicion.

He held up two pages in the air, one typed and one handwritten. "Look at this. The eleven A.M. meeting doesn't list Brandon Shaw as an attendee, and the penmanship changes on the notes."

"What was the meeting?" Dora asked, reaching for the page. "Hmm, it was a personnel matter. It makes sense that they'd have limited the attendees to the bare minimum. What are the chances Brandon knew the schedule in advance?"

"Fairly good," Harris guessed. "Given he's the clerk, he likely had to circulate the agenda and make sure everyone knew when to arrive. But whether he and Mary conspired to both be there, and be free at the same time, is a different matter."

Dora set the papers aside and rose from her seat. "There's nothing for it. We've got to search his flat."

"Now?" Rex asked, looking up at her. "It's broad daylight."

"And Brandon is at work," she countered. "This may be the only chance we get. If Harris and the twins come along to act as look-outs, I'm sure we can do it."

Rex didn't waste his breath arguing with her. Dora had that mulish expression on her face that signalled intractability. He got up and Harris followed suit.

Only Inga remained where she was. "No sense in all of us traipsing across town. I'll stay here, in case anything else comes up."

Dora rang for Nonna Matilda. Despite her grandmotherly appearance and never-ending offers of food, the woman's true responsibility was to provide support for their spy missions. Dora outlined what they needed to do.

"Let me think," Nonna Matilda said, tapping a finger against her chin. "Delivery services works for one person, but there are too many of you for that. Wait! I've got it. Repair and renovations are a constant phenomenon here in Rome. No one will think anything of it if you turn up with the excuse to fix something. Will that work?"

Dora hurried over and gave the older woman a warm embrace. "You are a genius. Lucky for us, you loaned your skills to the British government rather than creating a mafia of your own."

"My cousin Vito has a construction business. I'm sure he can loan us some materials." Nonna Matilda sent the men into the attic again, this time instructing them to find a box of jumpsuits normally favoured by tradesmen. "You can pretend to be electricians. I've got tool belts in the storage shed. Vito can add in some wire and you'll be all set."

It took the remainder of the morning for Nonna Matilda to make all the arrangements. In the early afternoon, when most Italians paused for a rest, the group of British spies met in the shed to gather their tools.

Besides screwdrivers and wire cutters, Dora added a lockpicking set. When they were ready to go, Rex asked Dora what was the plan.

"Brandon Shaw's flat is number 1C. I'd wager that's on the first floor. If we get in a bind, that's not so high that we can't go out a window. Therefore, Harris, I'd like you to stay out front. Archie, you cover the back of the building. If anything comes up, Basil, you can dash up the stairs to let us know."

They parked the lorry they'd borrowed in plain view of the building. While the men unloaded their boxes of tools and wire, Dora set off in a purposeful stride to locate the rear entrance. Dressed as she was in men's clothing, with a flat cap covering her hair, Rex had to admit she gave every appearance of being a young man.

A few interminably long minutes later, she opened the front door. "Sorry about the wait. The last time someone oiled the rear lock, Caesar Augustus was emperor."

Harris remained by the lorry, keeping busy by sorting through the various bits and bobs left inside the bed. Rex and the twins followed Dora into the building.

The door opened to a narrow corridor, with a staircase leading up along the right wall. Near the door was a battered wooden table littered with restaurant flyers and newspapers. Numbered cubicles hung above the table, each one labelled with a different flat number and name. 1C had the name Shaw next to it, but the letter space was empty.

Again, Rex and Dora made no effort to hide their presence. Real tradesmen were hardly worried about disturbing other tenants. Their tool belts clanked and footsteps echoed as they climbed the stairs to the first floor. A glance at the numbering indicated the flat they sought was off to their right.

Rex provided cover while Dora picked the lock. Not that it mattered. If there was anyone else at home, they did not come out to investigate the noise. When the latch turned and the door swung open, Rex hitched up his belt and followed Dora inside. He closed the door and engaged the lock before turning around to see the room.

Rex had expected to find a single room, similar to the boarding houses so common in London. Instead, this was a proper flat. Rex found himself in a foyer of sorts. The narrow stairs on the back wall leading into a loft explained the low ceiling in this part of the room.

Dora had walked ahead, going into the sitting room. She pulled back the curtains on the double-height windows. The daylight revealed a leather sofa, wingback chair, table and chairs for two, and a line of bookcases. Cheap prints graced the walls, standing in stark contrast to the fading fresco decorating the ceiling.

"Fancy flat for a clerk's salary," Dora commented. "If we didn't know that the embassy owned the building, I'd be certain our Mr Shaw had an unexplained source of income."

"Instead, this must be part of the compensation packet for living at the ambassador's beck and call." Rex pulled a face. "I wonder how much time Brandon actually spends here."

With that question in mind, Rex examined the flat more closely. There wasn't a single thing out of place. Shaw had even aligned the newspapers stacked on the end table. The shelves were filled with books arranged in alphabetical order by the author's last name, just like in a library. A single notepad and pencil sat beside a telephone, ready to be used should a request come in.

"We'll have to be very careful to put everything back the way we found it," Dora commented, her mind going in the same direction. "I'll take this room. You check the others."

Rex turned around and walked into a small alcove off the foyer. It turned out to be a kitchenette. He found boxes of cereal and dried pasta next to jars of fruits and vegetables, all ordered by size. In front was a string of cured meat. Again, the obsessive tidiness was in evidence. There wasn't a stray crumb anywhere.

The next doorway revealed a private bathroom. There was nothing to see other than a single towel, toothbrush, razor, and a bar of soap. Inside the medicine cabinet, Rex found a bottle of hair oil and a brush free of stray hairs. At the rate they were going, they'd have nothing to show for their efforts.

"I'm going up to the loft," Rex announced.

Dora glanced up from the book she was searching and waved him on. The stairs were so narrow that Rex had to stay on the balls of his feet. He emerged into a shadowed loft with a low ceiling and single bed. The bedding was pulled tight and tucked in at the corners with the precision of a seasoned soldier.

Time at the front lines had drilled into men like Rex and Brandon the necessity of putting everything in its place. When Rex had returned home, he had embraced the freedom of disarray. To him, seeing a pair of trousers tossed over the back of a chair reminded him he was no longer at war.

Brandon Shaw had gone the opposite direction. He'd clung to the incessant need for order, not allowing himself even an inch of imperfection. Rex struggled to match that image with the picture of a traitor and murderer. How could a man still living under the edicts of central command flaunt the rule of law so flagrantly?

Unless it was his dedication to order that enabled him to

keep his misdeeds hidden. Only a man this precise could cover up a crime.

With this thought in mind, Rex approached the bedside table. He turned on the lamp and opened the drawer. The only thing inside was a pencil.

He let that be and did a swift check under the mattress. Again, nothing. He smoothed the covers back into place, leaving no trace. That left the wardrobe.

The door opened smoothly on well-oiled hinges. Rex glanced inside each of the three drawers, noting the exacting order of undershirts, socks, and pants. The hanging clothes were no different. Brandon owned one formal suit, two shirts, two pairs of trousers, and two empty hangers.

Rex turned back to the bed. He dropped to his hands and knees and peered underneath. A quick swipe with his hand confirmed his suspicions. He'd seen enough. He stood back up and hurried down the stairs, taking care not to slip on the smooth wooden surface. Dora was waiting by the front door.

"Find anything?" he asked.

"Only one thing, and I'm not even sure it counts a clue. Remember Mr Tomlins — the ambassador's traitorous private secretary? Brandon had a copy of his obituary tucked inside the pages of a book. It's odd, but on its own, I'm hesitant to attach too much meaning to it."

"Maybe my findings will change your mind. Or, I should say, it is what I didn't find. The travelling case Brandon stored under his bed is missing, along with at least one change of clothes. I also didn't find his passport. Unless I'm mistaken, Brandon Shaw is on the run."

Chapter 20
The Repeat Offender

D ora agreed with Rex's logic, but she had to make sure. After pulling the drapes shut, they hurried downstairs to where Basil was waiting.

"Get Archie and meet us out front," Dora instructed.

Despite his muscular stature, Basil's footsteps hardly made a sound. Years of growing up in London's slums had taught him the importance of moving silently. It made him a great footman and an even better pickpocket. In Dora's unusual household, those two skills were equally valuable.

Out front, they helped Harris reload the spools of wire he'd set out as part of their disguise while telling him what they'd learned.

"What do you want to do next?" he asked once the twins had caught up. "We can go home and ring the embassy."

Dora contemplated the suggestion before striking it from her list. "If he's there, I don't want to risk him running when we call. Better to catch him unawares. Besides, for all we know, there may be a perfectly logical reason he is going away."

Rex looked down at their tradesmen's uniforms. "We can

hardly all go in like this. Our electrician cover won't hold up to any kind of scrutiny."

Dora glanced around, searching for inspiration. She got it when she spotted the fruit and vegetable market. "Wait here. I'll be right back."

With no explanation, she dashed across the street, nearly getting run down by a passing cyclist, and into the shop. She emerged a few minutes later with a wrapped box in hand. After crossing back, taking better care to check this time, she handed it to Archie. She finished up with a folded slip of paper.

"One delivery addressed to Brandon Shaw. We'll drop you off a short distance away and you can take this inside. Tell the guards that he has to sign for the package. You cannot leave it with anyone but the addressee."

Archie pocketed the paper and then climbed into the back of the lorry. "What do I do if he is there?"

"Leave the box with him and then hurry back to tell us. We'll decide our next steps after that."

Rex and Basil joined him in the back and they set off. On the drive over, Harris asked Dora what she'd put in the box, and how she'd explained it to the market owner.

"I nearly forgot I was supposed to be a man. The first thing I saw was a shelf of pasta. I grabbed several packets and asked him to box them for me. When he looked at me askance, I said I wanted to show the woman I was serious about providing for our future."

"Quick thinking," Harris said with a chuckle. "If the clerk isn't there, I'm laying claim to the box. I'll give it to Inga and see how she reacts to the line."

"As long as you make sure I see her reaction, you have a deal."

Dora told Harris where to pull over. Archie jumped out of the lorry bed and strode down the pavement, whistling while he walked. From where they'd parked, Dora watched him go through the gate and into the building.

Dora settled in to wait, but Archie was back before she found a comfortable seating position in the borrowed vehicle. He had the box in his hands and a concerned expression on his face.

"He left for lunch and has yet to return. I asked if there was someplace else I could take the delivery, but the front desk guard said no. Mr Shaw is supposed to be in all day."

Dora was out of bright ideas. It was time to regroup. She told Archie to hop back in and directed Harris to take them to Nonna Matilda's.

It was just their poor luck that traffic had slowed to a crawl. Shops were reopening after the long lunch break. Dora saw all of humanity pass her by while they inched along the crowded roads. Housewives ran errands, clutching school children by the hand. Men and women called to them from their market stands, hawking their goods to all who passed by. Interwoven between them came the tourists, their noses buried in maps and guidebooks rather than glimpsing the surrounding sites. The desperate poor took advantage of their inattention to lift a pocketbook before disappearing into the chaos.

The scene only reminded Dora of their immense challenge. How could they hope to find one man in all this? A man who was a veritable stranger, no less. What did Dora know of him? He worked hard, lived simply, and his rooms showed little evidence of friends. Dora wasn't content to give up, no matter how difficult the challenge was. She trusted herself and her friends to find him.

They arrived at Nonna Matilda's house, dripping with sweat from their time in the sun. Dora took one look at the men and declared the necessity of a brief pause. "Clean up, change into your own clothes, and let's meet on the terrace. We can strategise over glasses of fresh juice."

She didn't need to issue her orders twice. Archie and Basil headed for the guest house. Dora called out the request for refreshments on her way through the kitchen. Then she, Rex, and Harris took the staircase at the rear of the house to reach their rooms.

Less than a quarter of an hour later, looking decidedly more like themselves, Dora and the men settled around the table. She noted with pleasure that Cynthia had joined her brothers. Clark was still out with Edith and Prudence. That left one person unaccounted.

"Harris, did you not ask Inga to come along?"

"She wasn't in our room. She's probably reading something in the library. Shall I go fetch her?"

Dora waved for him to keep his seat. Nonna Matilda was on her way out with a tray of salted snacks. After she thanked her for the restorative treats, she asked her to send Inga their way.

"Signora Inga isn't here. She received a message not long after you left and headed out shortly thereafter."

"Did she say where she was going?"

Nonna Matilda shook her head, making the tendril framing her face sway. "No, and I didn't ask. She said she wouldn't be gone long. Do you want me to send her here when she returns?"

Dora replied yes and Nonna Matilda left them to their discussions. Dora, however, was too distracted to note the start of the conversation. Who would have sent Inga a note and where would she have gone? Had something happened to Edith and Clark?

The rational side of her mind argued that if something terrible had happened, Inga would have left word. The more inventive side worried about Inga being on her own in a foreign city.

Rex touched Dora's arm to get her attention. "Caledonia's home alone. She probably invited Inga over for tea."

His explanation made so much sense that Dora wondered why she hadn't thought of it on her own. Thus reassured, she turned her mind to their quandary.

"He took a change of clothes and his passport. We should check all the ways of getting out of the country. He's got enough of a lead on us we're unlikely to catch him straight away. Best case, we can figure out where he is going."

Harris added his agreement. "We'll need a list of the train stations. Someone should also check the port."

"This will be a lot to cover on our own. Can we ask the Carabinieri for help?" Rex asked.

Dora considered the question, but put it aside for the moment. "We don't have enough evidence to say for sure Brandon is guilty. And if he is betraying our country, we don't want word of that leaking out. Let's make a list of all the places we should check. We can always ask Nonna Matilda to recruit people from her network."

Archie went inside to retrieve maps from the study. Meanwhile, Dora moved into his seat to sit next to Cynthia. While the men reviewed the transport options, Dora and Cynthia sketched a drawing. Between Dora's keen eye and Cynthia's artistic skills, they drafted an excellent likeness. Cynthia rapidly sketched a few more, so each of them had a copy.

They were all so intent on their work, they failed to hear Clark come home until he bellowed a hello.

"What ho, old chaps? Any news?"

Rex hurried through an explanation of why they were planning a manhunt through Rome and the surrounding area.

Clark took off his coat and pushed up his sleeves. "What can I do to pitch in?"

They'd already included Clark on the list of assignments. What they were missing, however, was someone to act as the central point of command. Inga was ideally suited for that role. What they needed most was for her to return.

Dora turned to Clark. "I know you just came from there, but would you mind taking the car back to Rex's grandmother's house and picking up Inga?"

Instead of rushing to execute the request, Clark tilted his head to the side. "Inga isn't at Lady Rockingham's home."

Dora and Harris both stilled. They asked, almost in unison, "Are you sure?"

Clark frowned. "I'm positive. I popped in to say hello to Caledonia. She had shortly returned from her afternoon lesson. If Inga was there, I'd have seen her."

Sirens blared in Dora's mind. She turned tail and strode off to find Nonna Matilda. The older woman was in the kitchen, rolling out pasta for their evening meal.

Dora cleared her throat to get her attention. "Inga still hasn't returned. I don't suppose you know whether she left the message behind."

Nonna Matilda stopped what she was doing and reached for a cloth to wipe her hands. "This is not like Signora Inga. Let me help you look."

They first checked the drawing room, where Inga had been sitting when the message came in. A thorough search of the bin, tables, and even between the sofa cushions failed to reveal the note.

"Maybe in her room? She went upstairs before she left."

Again, Dora trailed behind Nonna Matilda. Despite her age, the older woman was still spry enough to hurry up the stairs.

At first glance, the room offered no help. Other than a book on the bedside table, all the other surfaces were neat and clean.

Dora's stomach clenched as her concern rose to proper worry. If Inga pocketed the note, they'd have no clue where to find her.

But Inga was smarter than that. She'd warned Dora enough times not to rush off like a fool. The note had to be there somewhere.

"Ecco!" Nonna Matilda emerged from the dressing room, waving a small envelope in the air. "This is the one I brought to her. I recognise the handwriting."

Dora took the proffered letter. Like Nonna Matilda, she also recognised the distinct shape of the G in Inga's name. Her hand trembled so badly she almost tore the letter inside in her rush to get it free.

"Sister Inga, I am in desperate need of help. You saved my life once before. Please, I must beg you to do so again."

The note included the name and address of a cafe in the city centre. It was unsigned, but Dora didn't need a name to identify the sender. There was only one person in Rome who referred to Inga as sister.

Inga had gone to meet with Brandon Shaw. She clearly hadn't expected to be away for long. Nor had she read the note as a threat.

The worst of it was, in Inga's shoes, Dora would have done the same. Inga knew that Dora and the others were searching Brandon's flat. She'd have agreed to the meeting if for no other reason than to keep him from returning home.

But now, she'd failed to return. Dora whispered a fervent prayer that there was a logical reason for her absence. But she couldn't tamp down the fear that Inga was at risk.

After all, if Brandon had murdered one English woman, what was to stop him from doing so again?

Chapter 21
The Secret Message

Rex surveyed the maps spread across the terrace table. There was so much ground to cover, and their lack of familiarity made the situation worse. Even with the help of Nonna Matilda's local network, they were still facing a monumental task. He almost wished he was searching for a needle in a haystack. At least then he'd only have one place to look.

Dora's shouts broke Rex's concentration. She practically flew through the door and onto the terrace, clutching a piece of paper in hand. Her face was unusually pale and her voice held a sharp edge of terror.

"He has Inga!" she blurted.

Harris lurched sideways. "Who has Inga?"

"Brandon Shaw." She thrust the paper into Rex's hand. "See, it says Sister Inga. That's how he addressed her the day she bumped into him on the street. It has to be him."

While Rex and Harris scanned the contents of the note, Clark was busy scratching his head.

"I don't understand. Why would Brandon Shaw contact Inga? And why would he call her sister?"

"She was a nurse at the front, and apparently, she cared for him after his injury."

"Never mind that now," Harris said, cutting in. "Why did he contact her? Do you think this request was genuine, or did he know she was connected to the investigation?"

"Unfortunately, we won't have the answer to that until we find them. Nonna Matilda sent Giuseppe to start the car. If we squeeze, we've got space for four. Who wants to come along?"

Harris stepped forward first, and Rex was close behind. While Archie and Basil debated between themselves, Clark stepped into the breach.

"I'm coming," he announced in a no nonsense tone. "If we need to split up to search, I'm best suited to go to the embassy with a request for help."

No one argued with his well-made point. Harris took the front seat next to the driver. Rex waited for Dora to slide into the middle of the rear bench seat before getting in. With some careful shifting and little regard for personal space, he and Clark closed the doors.

For once, Rex didn't complain about Giuseppe's driving. The old man had terrified him before, but this time, his confidence on the road was to their benefit. He zipped in and out of traffic with ease, narrowly avoiding a multitude of accidents. He stopped the car on the nearest side of the piazza and pointed toward the cafe at the other end.

Harris waited for no man. He leapt out of the car and took off like a shot. Rex and Clark had fought in too many battles to follow in his footsteps. The men exchanged glances while Dora got out.

"We need to cover all the exits," Rex said.

Clark nodded. "If he bolts, there are too many directions in which he could run. I'll take the back. You and Dora can watch the square."

Rex and Dora quickly agreed with the proposal and the three split to go their separate ways.

Rex skirted the left side of the piazza, keeping half an eye on Dora as she did the same on the right. The threat of danger and fear for Inga caused Rex's heart to beat faster. Yet, time moved like treacle. He was tossed back to his years at the front, where every rock and tree might hide an enemy. The shouts of playing children and the dull hum of passersby faded away. His steps slowed as he passed a wooden planter with flowering bushes. A flicker of movement between the leaves caught his eyes. Someone was there. At the last second, he lurched sideways to grab the hidden threat.

His hands landed on fluffy fur and a rough tongue licked his wrist, leaving a trail of wetness behind. Instead of finding an enemy soldier, he'd captured an overly friendly terrier leashed to the planter base.

He patted the dog on its head and straightened up, dusting himself off. He glanced around to check whether anyone had noticed. Only one person looked his way. Dora. She had a hand over her mouth to control her mirth.

He motioned for her to keep going and turned his gaze back to the cafe. If nothing else, he'd given Dora a brief respite from worrying about her best friend.

A sharp whistle caught his attention. Harris was standing in front of the cafe. His stony face told Rex everything. Inga wasn't inside.

Dora reached Harris first, but Rex was close enough behind to hear her words.

"Not there?"

"No sign of her or your clerk. I checked the kitchen, the toilettes, and the underground stockroom."

Dora took a deep breath and squared her shoulders. "We'll

find her. One of you get Clark while I go speak with the waitstaff. Perhaps someone remembers them."

Harris was too antsy to keep still, so he offered to fetch Clark. That left Rex to accompany Dora.

The cafe was larger than it appeared from out front. A well-stocked bar and long counter took up much of the space, leaving room for only a few round tables. Off to the side was an arched doorway leading to a spacious back room. There, Rex counted a dozen tables before he gave up. Every single one of them was occupied.

"Buonasera!" A suited waiter beamed at them, menus in hand. "Would you like a table? An aperitivo? We have an extensive cocktail menu."

Dora pulled the sketch of Brandon from her pocket and unfolded it. "We were supposed to meet someone here, but we got stuck in traffic. I don't suppose you saw him? There would have been a woman with him. Auburn hair, blue dress, a little taller than I am."

The waiter shook his head. "I'm sorry, signora, but I cannot help. I came on shift ten minutes ago. You can ask the others if you'd like."

The woman behind the counter scrunched her brow and said the man in the sketch was vaguely familiar, but that was all. So many people passed through the cafe. She couldn't even be sure she'd seen him that day.

Dora kept going. She and Rex remained close to the bar, stopping the waiters and waitresses when they came to put in a drink order. It was the fourth person they stopped who gave them some good news.

The woman rested her tray on the counter and wiped a line of sweat from her brow. She took the paper and studied it carefully while Dora added a description of Inga. "They were here. Left half an hour ago." She glanced at the clock. "Seven

PM already? Might have been more like an hour ago. Before the dinner crowd arrived."

She moved to go, but Dora halted her. "Can you remember anything about them? How did the woman act? Was she nervous, scared, happy?"

The waitress's smile dropped. "Bad relationship? You don't need to explain. I wish I could help, but you see how it is here. We were short-staffed until Stefano showed up for his shift. I was run off my feet. You're lucky I even remember them."

"Did they leave anything behind? A note? Did the woman say anything on her way out?"

"I didn't see them leave. They left money on the table while I was serving others."

Her answer dashed Rex's hopes, but Dora was more tenacious.

"Where did they sit?"

The waitress pointed toward a two-seater table on the far side of the back room. "Someone else is there now."

Dora let the waitress go and then told Rex to go outside and find the others. "I'll be out in a few minutes."

Rex knew better than to ask questions. He sought her hand and squeezed it for luck before heading for the door. Harris and Clark stood out front.

Harris's face was unusually pale, but his eyes glittered with the hint of a threat. If Brandon Shaw had hurt Inga in any way, Harris would make him pay for it.

But there was still the matter of finding them. Harris had too much nervous energy to stand still. He rocked from side to side, moving like a boxer preparing to launch himself at an opponent.

Rex began speaking, mostly to keep Harris from running off. "This looks bad now, but there is an upside."

Clark gave Rex a sharp glance. "What's that?"

"We can safely assume that Brandon doesn't have any outside help. After all, if there was someone ready to lend a hand, would they countenance Brandon bringing along a hostage?"

"That's an excellent point."

"Don't celebrate yet," Harris countered. He stood still long enough to make a point of his own. "We have too many unknowns. Does Brandon know Inga is connected to you and Theodora? Is he planning to use her to keep us from arresting him?"

"We'll find out soon enough," Dora said from behind. She strode into the middle of their discussion, clutching a paper napkin in her hand. "I found this under the seat cushion. I recognise Inga's handwriting."

Harris grabbed the thin paper. "Lions? That's all she wrote?" He flipped it over and growled at the blank side. "What does that mean?"

"Thrown her to the lions?" Rex ventured.

"She's gone to the zoo?" Clark guessed.

Dora huffed and took the paper back. "He's taken her to the Colosseum! It's not far from here. The ancient Romans kept caged beasts underneath it, including lions."

Clark wrinkled his nose. "Would Inga be so obtuse in her clue?"

"Yes," Harris, Rex, and Dora answered in unison.

Clark blinked at the vehement replies. "Right then. I guess that's where we're going next."

"Not alone," Dora said, stopping them all in their tracks. "The tunnels under the Colosseum are a maze. It will take us forever to search on our own. We need help, and I'm sure Nonna Matilda can drum up some. Harris and Rex, we'll go to the Colosseum. Clark, you take the car, go back to the house, and tell her what we know. Come and meet us as soon as you can."

Clark clicked his heels together and gave a military salute. Rex fought back a smile as he watched his friend depart. His brief flare of amusement wasn't to last. Harris's frantic need to get his wife back consumed them all.

"How far away is the Colosseum from here?" Harris asked.

"A fifteen-minute walk," Dora replied.

Harris growled in frustration. "That's too long. All of this is taking too long."

Rex sensed Harris was on the edge of a breakdown. He couldn't blame the man. If the situation was reversed, he'd conquer the world if that was what was required to keep Dora safe.

Just as she'd do the same for him.

Rex scanned the piazza, stopping on a pair of young men cycling through the middle of the square. He waved his hand to flag them down and asked for Dora's help with translating.

"Ask them if we can buy their bicycles," he instructed before turning to Harris to ask him if he had any money on him. Together, they had a fair amount of Lira folded in their wallets. Certainly much more than the two old bicycles deserved.

The young men could hardly believe their luck at being offered such a substantial sum for their old bikes. They happily took the money and scampered off on foot without a backward glance.

Harris claimed one bicycle while Rex threw his leg over the other. Dora hopped up to sit upon the handlebars. She used one hand to hold her precarious position while indicating directions with the other.

Rex chose not to think about how close they came to getting into an accident on the way to the ancient monument. It was testament to the skills of Rome's drivers that they avoided being hit. Only five minutes after leaving the cafe, they spotted the grey stone monument looming at the end of their road.

Rex squeezed tight on the brakes and eased the bike to a stop. Dora jumped down and smoothed her skirt. Rex and Harris didn't bother securing the bicycles. They'd served their purpose.

Before them, the Colosseum dominated the landscape. Two thousand years earlier, it had been home to bloodthirsty crowds watching men and women fight to their death. Now, criminals exploited its underground warrens for their own ill purposes.

Brandon Shaw had chosen his hiding place well. While they searched for their dear friend, there'd be no one to keep Brandon from escaping.

Chapter 22
The Lion's Roar

D ora cast her mind back to her recent visit. Although they hadn't toured the underground tunnels, she recalled that some were visible from the stands. She told Rex and Harris to follow before hurrying over to the ticket stand.

"Signori, you will have to keep your visit short," the ticket seller warned. "The monument closes in less than half an hour. It is not safe to be inside after dark."

Not safe for the average visitor, but Dora trusted Nonna Matilda to find them a suitable escort. For now, they could at least rule out the upper floors of the Colosseum.

There was no line at the entrance. Dora showed their tickets and the uniformed employee waved them through with a second warning about the closing time. Rex and Harris kept close behind as she led them inside the ancient stone walls.

The sprawling site held Dora's best friend captive. Dora, Rex, and Harris lost no speed, making their way to the nearest stairwell. The only problem they encountered was finding a way up, given everyone else was coming down.

Harris shouted a warning, and the crowd parted, leaving a

narrow path for them to pass. They emerged on the first level above the old floor and rushed to the nearest viewing platform.

Once again, the sheer size and scale of the Roman ruin took Dora's breath away. Built to hold seventy-thousand attendees, the venue dwarfed anything in England. Searching every square inch of the monstrosity would take more time than they could afford.

They had to be clever.

Dora clapped her hands to get the men's attention. "Rex, you take the stands to our right. Harris, you search the ones to our left. I will stay here in case they go past."

"What about the tunnels you mentioned?" Harris asked.

"We can't search those without a guide. We'll do what we can until Clark gets here with more help."

Despite what she said out loud, Dora held little hope they'd locate Inga so easily. However, she also knew the frustration of standing still when your heart urged you to move. This, at least, would keep all three of them occupied.

Dora's eyes traced the various levels, her eyes focusing on every flicker of motion. More than once, she saw Rex or Harris run past an opening into the stands. Each time, they hurried forward, waved at her, and shook their heads. Still, they stayed until the Colosseum staff forced them to exit the grounds.

Clark was waiting outside, accompanied by a well-dressed Italian man and two burly bodyguards. Based on the way Clark continued to cast nervous glances at his companions, Dora suspected there was more to them than met the eye.

Dora latched onto the arms of Rex and Harris, encouraging them to slow their steps and catch their breath. For her part, she wiped all traces of fear from her face and replaced it with the cool exterior that had always served her well.

The well-dressed man stepped forward and offered Dora his hand. Although the daylight was rapidly fading, Dora noted his smooth, tan skin, silk pocket square, and hard eyes. His mouth turned up in a smile, but his sharp gaze never lost its edge.

"Buonasera, Signora Laurent," he said.

If Dora had to guess, this man must be one of Italy's famous mafia dons. It made sense. Given the tunnels were a hotbed of criminal activity, who better to guide them than someone everyone feared?

When Dora slid her hand in his, he pulled her close and kissed her on both cheeks in the traditional Italian greeting. The sandalwood oil in his hair swamped her nose. She pulled back, but he kept a tight hold of her hand.

"I am Mario Sinopoli, from the Sinopoli family. Nonna Matilda indicated you need access to the tunnels. My associates here, Guido and Giacomo, will act as your guides on two conditions."

Dora steeled herself. No matter what the cost, she'd willingly pay it if it meant getting Inga back safely. She was less sure that Rex, Harris, and Clark would keep mum.

"What are your conditions?"

"The first is that you remain silent about anything you come across during your journey. As far as the rest of the world is concerned, you were never there. Should you break this vow, you may make another visit under much less pleasant circumstances."

Dora agreed to the condition with no hesitation. The possibilities for his second request had her worried. She'd been around enough to know that the families rarely acted out of kindness. Even Nonna Matilda, as well-connected as she was, could do no more than get Mario Sinopoli to show up.

"And the second condition? Is there something we can do for you?"

Signore Sinopoli glanced around, checking who else might be listening. He motioned for Dora to come closer. She forced her feet into motion, inching forward until he could whisper in her ear.

"If anyone asks, I demanded your help with trade arrangements with my counterparts in England. In truth, my request is much more personal. Nod if you understand."

Dora bobbed her head.

"Nonna Matilda makes the best tiramisu in all of Italy. If you promise me, you can get her secret recipe, I will guarantee safe passage for you and your friends."

Relief swamped over Dora, racing down her spine until her knees felt weak. It took all her concentration to keep any trace of humour from her face and tone.

She whispered back, "I will do you one better, Signore Sinopoli. As soon as we locate my lost friend, I promise Nonna Matilda will personally visit your chef to not only share her recipe but also to demonstrate how to execute it to perfection."

Signore Sinopoli stepped back and met her eyes head-on. A moment passed, and finally he released her hand. "We have an agreement." He muttered a command to his guides and then left without another word.

Guido and Giacomo unbuttoned their coats, giving Dora a glimpse of the pistols strapped to their waists. They squared their granite shoulders and pushed forward, leaving Dora and the others to follow.

Rex and Harris tossed Dora anxious glances, no doubt worried about what promise Mario Sinopoli had extracted. "Trade relations," she murmured.

The men weren't fooled. Such an obvious request required no secrecy. In the end, Dora whispered a promise to tell them all later.

Signore Sinopoli's guards, Guido and Giacomo, circled the monument. Although they wore custom-tailored suits, the fabric of their jackets strained to contain their bulging biceps and broad shoulders. Despite their size, they moved with the nimble feet of trained boxers.

The Colosseum grounds had emptied of all tour guides and staff. Metal gates blocked the entryways. The few remaining tourists gave their group a wide berth. Dora ignored them all and searched the exterior for any sign of the tunnel shafts.

She needn't have bothered. The bulky guards pointed them toward a shadowy hole on the far side of the grounds. They followed a dirt ramp down to a locked gate. Guido produced a key and made quick work of removing the lock and chain. Inside, the guards located a pair of oil lanterns. They lit the wicks and motioned for the others to keep up.

Dora almost wished the dark tunnels were silent. Instead, the lanterns cast ghastly shadows on the crumbling stone arches and walls. The pungent smell of mildew reminded Dora of rotting wood. Rodents scurried out of their way. A high-pitched screech made them all halt in their tracks.

"I gatti," Guido explained. "Cercano i topi."

Dora searched the surrounding area for any signs of Rome's stray cats. They numbered in the thousands and made their homes in the ancient ruins. Dora watched her feet as much to keep from stumbling over the rough floor as to avoid bumping into the modern day beasts.

The tunnels branched off from one another. As they passed, Dora caught the faint whisper of voices and scuffles of movement. Cigar smoke floated on the breeze. She closed her ears against the thuds and cries for mercy. None of the voices were familiar, and all spoke Italian. Right now, saving Inga was her only priority.

Still, she couldn't stop wondering about the tunnels left unexplored. There were dozens of alcoves carved into the ground and lined with stones. Former cells for prisoners, waiting areas for gladiators, even wooden lifts for raising the caged animals. She edged closer to their guides and asked about the last tunnel they'd passed.

In a thick Roman accent, Guido offered an explanation. "That one is used by the Corvetti family. If someone has trespassed onto their ground, we'll hear about it soon enough. Signore Sinopoli instructed us to check the tunnels we use, and those considered common ground."

"It is a much smaller area," Giacomo added.

Dora conveyed the information to the others. For the first time, she believed they'd find Inga before daybreak.

Unfortunately, her positive outlook wasn't destined to last. An hour later, Guido pronounced them at the end.

"This is the last hiding spot," he explained, lifting his lantern high enough to light the far corners of the narrow recess. "No one has been in here for days. Look here at the dirt on the stones. The ground hasn't been disturbed."

Dora refused to admit defeat. She'd read the clue. Lions had to mean the Colosseum. It made no sense for Brandon to take Inga to a zoo. Where would they hide?

Clark scooted closer and wrinkled his nose. "What a horrid place this is. I can't imagine anyone willingly coming here to find sanctuary."

Dora's head flipped up. "What did you say?"

Clark took a half step back. "Horrid? Willingly?"

"No — sanctuary! Clark Kenworthy, you are an absolute darling!" Dora lifted on her toes and kissed Clark on the cheek. "I've been blind! We've all been blind!"

"Care to explain?" Rex asked, nudging Dora with his elbow.

"Yes, but first let's get back above ground." Dora rattled off instructions to the guards in Italian.

Getting out again was much faster. Guido and Giacomo didn't make a single error when leading them to the exit. They extinguished the lanterns, locked the gate, and then demanded an explanation.

"Signore Sinopoli is expecting payment for our time," Guido said. "You aren't planning on double-crossing him, are you?"

"Certainly not. Please tell him he will be paid in full as per our agreement before the week is out. He has my word." Dora opened her arms wide to encompass the others. "All our words."

Rex, Harris, and Clark were fit to be tied. They kept quiet long enough to get some distance from the bodyguards. As soon as they were on safe ground, Harris grabbed Dora's hand and pulled her to a stop.

"Where is Inga?" he demanded.

"If I'm correct, Inga is sitting in perfect safety, no doubt grumbling about our slowness," Dora replied, adding, "And justifiably so. We've had this all wrong from the start. Brandon didn't kidnap Inga."

Harris reared back. "He didn't?"

"No. In fact, I suspect Inga is behind our search. Think about it. If he was planning to kidnap her, would he tell her where they were going? She obviously knew their destination since she left a note."

"A note that was wrong," Harris countered. "She isn't in the Colosseum."

"Exactly! I misunderstood the reference to lions. When we visited the other day, our tour guide told us about the wild beasts kept caged beneath the Colosseum. That was the first thing that came to mind. But anyone could have interpreted the clue. Our Inga is much too sensible to leave behind something obvious. In our rush to save her, I forgot he also mentioned that there was someplace else where their roars might instil a sense of fear."

Harris's eyes grew wide. "Where?"

"In a prison. A prison that is now located beneath a church. When Clark said the word sanctuary, he reminded me of the tour guide's comment. What if Inga was attempting to detain Brandon, rather than the reverse?"

"Why would she do that?" Clark asked. "Why wouldn't she bring him home?"

Dora shrugged her shoulders. "We can ask her that when we find her."

Chapter 23
Safe From Harm

The group wasted no time travelling to their new destination. The church in question sat on the other side of the Roman forum. After a quick chat, the group agreed it would be fastest to flag down a taxi. They hurried to the nearest major road, where they chanced upon an empty taxi waiting at the corner.

Five minutes later, Rex had to ask Clark to pay the driver, after explaining he'd used all his funds to buy a pair of bicycles.

The church in question, San Giovanni dei Falegnami, took its name from Joseph, the famed carpenter father of Christ. Deep underneath the 17th century facade lay the ancient Mamertine Prison that, according to legend, had once hosted the disciples St Paul and St Peter.

With unerring steps, Dora swept past the entry to the underground prison chambers and instead hurried up the elegant, balustraded staircase leading to the church above it.

On the way over, Rex had feared another lengthy search, imagining a sprawling church complex. Instead, he found a narrow sanctuary lined with wooden pews. Overhead, carved wooden beams, heavily layered with gilt, glittered in the candlelight. His looked past the frescoed walls and marble statues. He took no notice at all of the distant altar. All his attention was on the straight back of the auburn-haired woman kneeling at the front pew.

"Inga!" Dora cried.

Inga took her time in rising to her feet. She slid out of the pew and into the aisle, where she placed her hands on her hips and stopped Dora with a glare. "What took you so long to get here?"

Rex couldn't stop the smile from spreading across his face as Dora ignored her friend's annoyed tone and swept her into a hug.

"Sister Inga?" a man gasped. "You know them?"

In his singular focus, Rex had overlooked the man sitting at the far end of the opposite pew. He rose now, his movements hesitant as he took in the faces around him.

It was Brandon Shaw. His moustache drooped, and his dishevelled hair revealed his hours of stress. Looking at him now, Rex asked how he could have ever imagined the man as a killer. His desperate message to Inga had been authentic. He begged for help, and Inga had provided.

Still, Rex and the others had a hundred and one questions for the pair.

Given the late hour, no one else was in the church. They collectively decided that the easiest thing to do was remain where they were.

Inga slid into the pew to sit beside Brandon, offering him her moral support. Harris claimed Inga's other side. He wrapped his arm around Inga's shoulders and pulled her close. In an unusual display of affection, he pressed a gentle kiss against her forehead.

Rex spotted a line of folding chairs leaning against the wall. He grabbed three and brought them over, offering one each to

Dora and Clark. In short order, they formed a tidy circle in the front of the quiet church.

Inga's expression softened as she lay a hand on Brandon's arm and gave it a reassuring squeeze. "I swear to you that my friends are worthy of your trust. They owe no allegiance to anyone in Rome and want nothing more than to uncover the truth. Please, tell them what you told me."

Brandon took a deep breath and began. "To help you understand, I need to go back in time. Three years ago, to be exact, when Donald Tomlins, the previous private secretary, died unexpectedly. I told you I packed his things and shipped them to his family. There is something I left out."

"Go on," Rex urged.

"Donald and I served in the same unit during the war. He suggested I come to Rome and even put in a good word for me. That's how I became a clerk. I wouldn't say we were friends, but we were friendly enough. He was more of a mentor than anything else.

"A few weeks before his death, he began acting strangely. I caught him glancing over his shoulder when we were out for a drink after work. I asked him what was wrong, but he said it was best I remained in the dark. I assumed he'd got into a spot of trouble with the locals — it happens, although the embassy does its best to sort that kind of thing out. But then he died... and well, nothing made sense."

Rex, Dora, Inga, and Harris nodded along, aware enough of the big picture to see how this might connect. Clark, however, was in the dark.

"What does that have to do with now?" he asked, shaking his head in confusion.

"After Donald's death, I took over his flat. Someone had searched through his things. At first, I assumed it was related to the inquiry into his death, but then I found an envelope taped to the underside of a kitchen drawer. Inside were two smaller envelopes. One was addressed to his family. The second envelope was bulkier."

"What was in it?" Rex asked.

Brandon shrugged. "I didn't have the nerve to open it."

Clark spluttered. "The nerve? In your shoes, I'd have ripped the envelope to get at the contents. You could have been in danger."

Brandon reared back. "I'm no fool! Look at me, man. I will forever bear the scars from the last time I rushed headlong into dangerous territory. When I looked at that envelope, Donald's warnings to stay out of it replayed in my mind. I heeded them. I posted the letter to his family and hid the other."

"Hid it where?" Dora asked this time.

"In the archives room at the embassy. I didn't want it anywhere near me, and there was little chance of it being discovered there. The room is packed to the rafters with old files and official documents."

Clark waved a hand to get everyone's attention. "I still don't see what this has to do with you running off now. Was Donald murdered?"

Brandon shrank in his seat. "I suspect so. I can't believe he'd kill himself. It made no sense! He had a family back in England. And he showed no hint of sadness or despair — only fear. But I put it out of my mind until someone else died. The last thing I expected was for the police to accuse the ambassador. After I heard, I found myself looking at Sir Francis differently. And from there, my thoughts returned to Donald. If Donald had been in trouble with the mafia, why not go to Sir Francis for help? He worked directly for the man!"

Clark leaned forward and growled, "Are you saying Sir Francis is guilty?"

Brandon nodded and then shook his head. "I don't know!

I'm so confused, but I can't make any other explanation fit. When you three showed up and started asking me questions, I panicked."

"We didn't consider you a suspect," Rex said in a reassuring tone. "Or, not at first anyway. You have to admit, you've acted suspiciously."

"It's because I'm terrified. Someone is out to pin this on me."

Clark didn't follow. "Why do you say that?"

"Because someone searched my office last night. They did their best to cover their tracks, but my things were out of place. They searched through my files and my desk. The only thing missing were the notes from the meeting on the day the murdered woman visited the ambassador's home."

"How do you know she was there?" Dora interjected.

"Because I saw her," Brandon hissed. "I stepped out to run an errand and crossed paths with her in the corridor. Imagine my shock when I saw her photograph in the newspaper under a headline about murder. Someone is planning to pin the crime on me, and I wasn't about to stick around and let it happen."

Harris leaned past Inga and glared at the clerk. "Why did you send a message to Inga, of all people?"

"I was desperate," he confessed. He raised his eyes to meet Inga's, revealing his anguish. "I needed help to get out of Italy. I didn't dare ask anyone at the embassy. When I ran into you on the street, it was as if fate took an active hand. I'm sorry for bringing you into this and scaring your friends. I realise now that all I've done is drag the rest of you into this situation. All our lives are at risk."

"Perhaps," Dora muttered. "But I wouldn't count us out yet. We've got ourselves out of plenty of scrapes over the years."

Brandon sat up. "You'll help me get away? You must leave with me!"

Rex hated to dash the man's hopes, but running away wasn't

an option. That was exactly what had led to this mess. One glance at Dora confirmed she felt the same. She had her hands balled into fists, where they rested on her knees. With her chin jutted out, she was the picture of determination.

She must be reeling from the news that Donald Tomlins's death wasn't as clear cut as it had seemed. She'd spend the next days kicking herself for not investigating further.

Three years ago, Dora had suspected Sir Francis of treason. Now, there was a chance that a double murder should be added to the list. But making charges this serious required solid proof.

Rex knew what they had to do.

"Brandon, the only way you'll ever be safe again is if we identify the real killer. Do you understand?"

Brandon gulped. "I... I guess so."

Rex held the man's gaze. "To do this, we need all the evidence we can get — including the envelope you hid in the archives. Tonight, you and I are going to pay a visit to the embassy. I will be with you the entire time. What do you say?"

Brandon stood up and squared his shoulders, wearing the grim-faced expression of a man heading into battle. "I don't want to spend the rest of my life looking over my shoulder. If you all have faith you can solve this riddle and put the real killer behind bars, then I'd be a fool to shun your offer to help. Lord Rex, I'm ready to leave as soon as you are."

Brandon leaned down and retrieved his travel case from where he'd stashed it under the pew. He handed it to Inga and asked her to keep it safe until his return.

Outside, Clark and Harris waved their arms until a taxi deigned to stop. Brandon climbed in first and slid across to make room for Rex. Dora caught Rex's hand and stopped him before he followed.

She threw her arms around his neck and hugged tight

against him. As much as he treasured the moment of tenderness, he quickly realised Dora had an ulterior motive.

She raised on her toes and whispered in his ear, "Last time I ignored my intuition. This time I intend to listen. If Sir Francis is behind any of this, I'm not leaving Rome until we can prove it."

Chapter 24
The Bribe

Nonna Matilda cried with joy when Inga walked through her front door. She pulled her into a tight hug and didn't let go until Dora intervened.

"Nonna Matilda, didn't you get our message? Inga was never in any danger."

The older woman huffed as she speared Dora with a glare. "I wasn't hugging her for her sake, but for my own. I was terrified!"

Inga patted their host on the arm and murmured an apology. Nonna Matilda agreed to forgive them all for scaring her if they would sit down and enjoy a meal. Although she posed it as an invitation to sate their hunger, her tone left no doubt that it was an ultimatum.

Dora shrugged her shoulders. "We can't do anything until Rex and Brandon return. And I don't know about anyone else, but wandering through the lower depths of the Colosseum has left me starving."

"And dirty!" Nonna Matilda exclaimed. "Change out of those clothes while I prepare the table."

In short order, Dora, Inga, Harris, and Clark claimed their

places around the large dining room table, all feeling much refreshed. They helped themselves to the various dishes of pasta, roasted vegetables, and cold salads, all served family-style. They passed around a basket of sliced bread and then dived in with little regard for proper manners. They were, quite simply, too hungry to pretend otherwise.

Rex returned with Brandon before the rest of the group reached dessert.

Clark dropped his fork when they walked into the dining room. "Back already? And empty-handed to boot! I take it you couldn't find the envelope."

Rex unbuttoned his jacket and pulled a sheaf of folded papers from the inner pocket. "Brandon found the envelope where he left it. I pulled some additional information while we were there."

Clark held out a hand, demanding Rex pass over the contents. He flipped through the pages before passing them along to Dora. "These are nothing more than meeting minutes from three years ago. Why did Mr Tomlins hide them away?"

Dora had the answer to that question, but she couldn't provide it. Those notes referenced private meetings between the ambassador and Italian politicians. It wasn't the notes themselves that caught her eye, so much as the blocks of unaccounted for time. On each occasion, Sir Francis asked Mr Tomlins to excuse himself to allow for more personal conversations.

It wasn't a smoking gun, but it was enough to convince Dora that she'd made a mistake in shutting down her original investigation into the ambassador. The irony was that if Mr Tomlins had left these meeting minutes in his files, she'd have found them during her searches. Instead, from where she'd stood back then, he'd appeared to be the leak within the embassy.

Mr Tomlins hadn't committed suicide. He must have done something to reveal his hand, and Sir Francis had acted swiftly to cover his tracks.

"Why did you bring back a personnel file?" Clark asked, drawing Dora's mind back to the present.

"It is Mr Tomlins's records. Of particular interest is the list of immediate family members. Check out his sister's name."

"Mary!" Clark exclaimed, drawing gasps from around the room.

"I took advantage of the embassy's telegraph machine to send a message to Lord Audley. I asked him to check Mary's age and whereabouts. Although, I'm afraid we already know the answer to the second question."

"Her name wasn't Mary Hunter, as we'd guessed," Dora muttered. "She was Mary, the hunter. If you're right, the Tomlins family has suffered a second, terrible loss."

Dora's stomach churned as the reality of her past failure set in. Worse yet, was the recognition that she was in no better position this time around. All she had were suspicions. It might be enough for Lord Audley to take quiet action behind the scenes, arranging for the removal of Sir Francis. Taking away the ambassador's career wasn't enough. Two people were dead, and he was almost certainly their killer.

She needed proof — solid, unassailable proof that would hold up in a court of law. All around her, the others spoke in low tones, arguing over what to do next. Dora needed quiet to concentrate. She murmured an apology and excused herself from the table.

Inga caught up with her at the top of the stairs. "Dora, wait. I've got something else you should see. I hid it in your room."

"Hid what?" Dora asked.

"A telegram. Remember the stack of messages I found in the rubbish when we searched the ambassador's office? There was one in there that stood out." Inga hurried over to Dora's dressing table and opened the top drawer. Sitting atop the jars of creams and powders was a plain white sheet of paper. "See what you think."

Dora's eyes skimmed over the page. The message was succinct. Addressed to Prudence, the sender thanked her for her message and asked her to keep in touch during her travels. It wasn't until Dora reached the name at the bottom that she figured out why Inga had saved the message.

"Sanderson! As in FR Sanderson, editor-in-chief of the Sunday Pictorial? Why would he send Prudence a telegram?"

Inga crossed the room to retrieve paper and a pen from the writing bureau. She jotted one line, then another. "Casper Eadmund is an anagram for Prudence Adams. I highly doubt that is an accident."

Dora gaped at her dearest friend. "Are you suggesting that Prudence Adams, one of society's wallflowers, is secretly London's most popular gossip columnist?"

Inga pointed to the page. "She has entrée into all the right circles, an ability to fade into the background, and a clever wit. She said herself that Sir Francis told her you were coming. Based on the date on the message in your hand, it appears she sent word to Sanderson straight away. Add on the matter of the anagram and you've got a watertight case for her being our secret columnist."

In her mind's eye, Dora replayed every conversation she'd had with Prudence in the last few days. She'd already concluded that there was more to Prudence than met the eye. But this?

Yet, like Inga, Dora could hardly argue with the mountain of evidence. If only she had a similar situation with Sir Francis. In that case, she'd be happy to give Prudence plenty of fodder for her next weekend column.

That thought led to another until she soon had a new plan in place.

"What we need is a confession - from Sir Francis, I mean."

Inga gave her a bland stare. "And what? He'll tell all to Prudence Adams?"

"Of course, not. However, if Miss Adams is as talented at sleuthing out hidden truths as we suspect, who's to say she couldn't pull the information from him?"

"I suppose it's possible," Inga agreed. "But how will you convince her to help?"

"I'll bribe her."

"With money?" Inga's skepticism was writ large across her face.

"With an exclusive," Dora replied. "If she will help us find justice for Donald and Mary Tomlins, I'll make sure she is the first to break the story. There's no time to lose. Be a doll and let Rex know what I'm doing. I'm going to see if Miss Adams would like to join me for a drive."

"At this hour?"

"Some types of business are best conducted under the cover of darkness."

Dora rang the ambassador's mansion and waited for Miss Adams to come on the line. Feigning tears, she explained that she'd had a falling out with Rex and desperately needed a distraction. After a couple of questions, Prudence was all too willing to accommodate the odd request, especially given the possibility of fresh gossip. That laid to rest any last doubts Dora had about Prudence's secret identity.

Nonna Matilda's driver had the motor car running. Dora slid into the back seat of the polished black Isotta Fraschini Tipo 8, which she'd come to love during their stay.

"Our first stop is the ambassador's villa. After we collect our passenger, drive around town until I tell you to stop."

Working in Nonna Matilda's household, the driver didn't question the strange request. He made haste to reach their destination. He came to a stop in front of the gate, waiting for the guards to wave them inside. Instead, the gated door swung open and Prudence came dashing out. Dora opened the car door from inside and motioned for her to get in. The driver barely gave Prudence time to settle before pulling into traffic.

Dora shifted in her seat to keep her face in the shadows. She didn't want Prudence to notice the lack of tears and reddened nose one would expect of an upset female.

There was no cause for concern. Prudence interpreted Dora's shyness as an attempt to hide the evidence of her emotional breakdown.

"Theodora, I'm so flattered you rang me in your time of need. How terrible it must be to find yourself in a foreign land while on the rocks romantically. Please, tell me how I can help calm your nerves."

Dora feigned a sniffle while she waited for the road to clear and for the car to pick up speed. She didn't want to give Prudence any possibility of escape.

When she judged the time right, she reached over and grasped Prudence's hand. "I've been under so much stress. You are so lovely to rush to my aid. There is one thing you could do that would make such a difference to me."

"Anything!" Prudence cooed.

Now that Dora was listening for it, she caught the hint of excitement in Prudence's voice.

Dora twisted in her seat so she could look Prudence in the eye. "You can coax a murder confession from Sir Francis."

"What?" Prudence reared back. "Why would I do such a thing? Furthermore, why would you ask? I thought you'd had a lover's quarrel."

Dora kept a tight hold on Prudence. "The only thing Lord

Rex and I have disagreed upon is how to prove beyond the shadow of a doubt that Sir Francis did indeed kill that young woman. He'd prefer to wait until we have undisputable evidence linking the ambassador to the crime. I have no interest in lingering in Rome indefinitely. Neither, I think, do you. Our interests align, dear Prudence. Or... should I say, Mr Eadmund?"

To give Prudence her due, the woman kept her cool in the face of Dora's subtle accusation. But her lack of confusion or outrage said more than her silence.

"Don't deny it. I have proof, not that I intend to use it. I have no plans to unmask you, or otherwise stand in your way."

"Then what is it you want?"

"I told you. Rex, Clark, and I have enough circumstantial evidence to link Sir Francis to the murdered woman. But circumstantial evidence isn't enough to ensure he pays for his crimes. I don't want him to be recalled and spend his days in a comfortable retirement. With a confession, the British government will have no choice but to issue a sentence which suits the crime."

"I see..."

Headlights from a passing car illuminated Prudence's face. She pursed her lips, but otherwise gave no hint as to her reply.

"Why me? Setting my pen name aside for the moment, why do you believe I'll do this? Sir Francis is a distant relation."

"No," Dora countered. "His wife is a distant cousin. I'm confident her family will find a way to redeem her reputation, especially given she isn't in Rome now. Plus, you've already illustrated your willingness to use information about Sir Francis for your gain. I read your last column — the one which referred to me and Rex. That was why I knew Casper Eadmund was in Rome."

"Drat," Prudence muttered.

Dora relinquished her hold on Prudence's hand. "You need not fear you'll be ill-used by this endeavour. If you help us by getting Sir Francis to confess in a setting where he can be overheard, we'll make sure you have exclusive rights to this story."

Prudence stilled. "All of it? Not just the confession? If I do this, I want Casper Eadmund to break the news every step of the way."

Dora stretched out her arm, offering Prudence her hand. "It's a deal. Shall we shake on it?"

Prudence raised her right hand and met Dora in the middle. This was no polite handshake in a society receiving line, but the hard grip of evenly matched opponents.

One day, Dora might kick herself for playing this card so soon. Now, however, the only regret she had was not stopping Sir Francis three years earlier.

Chapter 25
The Blind See All

I t was Sunday morning in Rome. The peal of church bells filled the air as the Eternal City's citizens heeded the call to worship. Traffic on the road was light, particularly in comparison with the foot traffic on the pavement. Well-dressed men and women walked arm in arm, counting the warm spring sunshine as another of life's blessings. Young boys kicked pebbles and pulled at their buttoned collars. The young women held their heads high and stepped carefully, emulating their mothers. Rex bit back a smile when he spotted a mischievous boy pulling on his sister's long braids before dashing out of reach.

There was much to be said for the simple life. Yet Rex felt no urge to join them. His desire to see the world while making a difference outweighed all other sentiments. While some feared chaos, Rex embraced it. He'd learned to love those escapes from the mundane.

He supposed that was why he'd agreed to go along with Dora's plan for catching their killer. She'd returned from her drive with Prudence and announced they had an ally. The plot to extract a confession was underway.

For anyone else, that news would be enough. But not Dora. She'd gathered the household and bade Brandon to join them as she outlined her vision for the next day.

Now, Rex sat in the back seat of the Isotta Fraschini, Clark at his side. Brandon, Harris, and Archie were making their way on foot.

Assuming all had gone well, Dora was already inside the ambassador's villa.

The complexity of the moving parts must have been weighing on Clark's mind. He cleared his throat to get Rex's attention. "Are you sure about this, old chap? Far be it from me to question your ways of working, but even you must see that this plan of Theodora's is a tad mad."

"If I've learned anything during our time together, it is that Theodora does nothing by half measures. She wants everyone involved in this matter to have closure. You must admit, she came up with an ingenious way to make it happen. And really, is this any worse than one of your infamous scavenger hunts?"

Clark opened his mouth to argue, but one glance at Rex's face had him swallowing his words instead. He wore the pained expression of a man forced to eat his least favourite dish.

Rex flashed him a bright smile. "Cheer up! Out of all of us, you have the simplest assignment. All you have to do is to be yourself!"

The driver steered the motorcar to a stop in front of a familiar red and green striped canopy. Across the street, in the shadow of the tall palm, a single rose lay against the stone wall. It marked the spot where Mary Tomlins had taken her last breath.

Rex suspected the woman responsible for placing the marker was the one he'd come to retrieve. Seated at a table in front of her family cafe was Signora Lucia Varotti. She'd borne witness to the crime. It was only fitting she be part of recording the murderer's confession.

As agreed, Clark moved into the front seat of the car, freeing space for her to join them. Rex called a hello and offered her his arm.

While Signora Varotti rose from her chair and gathered her handbag, her son emerged from inside the cafe. He put his hands on his hips and stared at Rex. The white apron covering his clothing did nothing to reduce the menace in his stance.

"Do you promise you will keep her safe?"

"Io prometto," Rex answered, in Italian. "She will come to no harm while in our company. I will stay by her side for the entire time."

Signora Varotti laid one hand on Rex's arm and raised her other to stop her son from further argument. "I am the mother and you are the child. Do you need another lesson about respecting your elders?"

The younger Varotti flushed and quickly hung his head in embarrassment. "No, Mamma. Tutto bene."

Signora Varotti nudged Rex toward the car. He opened the door and bade her to enter. By the time he rounded the car and took his seat, Signora Varotti was busy chatting with Clark.

"Mademoiselle Theodora came by and explained everything to me. You have no need to fear. I will play my part."

They arrived at their destination only a moment later. The guard stationed at the entrance to Sir Francis's home motioned for the car to stop. Clark got out to chat with him.

Clark had worn his most expensive suit and a haughty expression to match it. He drew himself up, stuck his nose in the air and issued a barrage of demands.

"New evidence has come to light suggesting someone snuck out of the villa grounds around the time of the murder. My colleague and I require your assistance with a detailed inspection."

The guard gave a nod of understanding. "Of course, my lord. Tell me how I can assist."

"Lord Reginald will take responsibility for interviewing the staff. You must accompany me on a full tour of the grounds."

At this, the guard shifted uncomfortably. "There are only two of us on duty today, my lord."

"Excellent, you can both attend me. Call your colleague, bar the front gate, and we can be on our way." Clark's voice rang with such authority that the guard had no choice but to comply. He waved the car forward and then closed the gate.

Clark's job was to distract the guards by leading them on a pointless search around the large property. With them occupied elsewhere, Harris and Archie would help Brandon sneak over the wall and cross unnoticed to the house. They had strict instructions about how to do so and where to position themselves for the next stage of the plan.

Rex told the driver to pull around to the carriage house and park the car. With relief, he noted Dora's driver had done the same. Dora had gone ahead, stopping to chat with Signora Varotti before arriving for a visit with Prudence. The parked car reassured him she was inside setting the stage.

Rex next did something no reputable member of the class would contemplate. He went to the servant's entrance and rapped on the door.

A girl, wearing a plain brown dress and white apron, opened the door. She took one look at Rex and Signora Varotti and promptly dropped the mixing bowl in her hands. Fortunately for them all, the bowl was empty. It did, however, cause so much of a clatter that the cook came running.

The woman was well-trained enough to know she was absolutely in over her head. She invited them into the kitchen and bade Rex and Signora Varotti to wait while she ran to fetch Mr Jenkins.

The staid English butler arrived a short while later, bursting into the kitchen in a surprising display of speed. He was utterly horrified to find a member of the upper class cooling their heels on the lower floors.

"Good heavens, Mrs Phipps! You could have at least shown Lord Reginald to my office!" he blurted, turning a blistering glare on the cook. The poor woman blubbered for a moment, before turning tail and disappearing into the cellars.

Under any other circumstances, Rex would have apologised for both the disturbance and the unorthodox behaviour. Today, however, he needed to keep the butler from cottoning on to what was happening on the main floor. He took a page from Clark's book, squared his shoulders, and adopted his most commanding tone.

"Mr Jenkins, I have brought Signora Varotti here for the next stage of our investigation. She believes she can identify the murderer based on their footsteps. Please line up every male member of staff so that she can listen to them walk.

"Now, my lord? The servants are busy with their last-minute tasks before their afternoons off."

Rex looked down his nose at the butler. "Are you questioning my request? A woman is dead. Surely the house can accommodate a minimum of interruption."

Jenkins's face turned to stone as he bit back any reply. Butler or not, it was not his place to question the actions of his betters, particularly when they were working on behalf of the Crown. Still, his eye twitched when Rex commandeered the use of the main below-stairs corridor.

"To save time, I'd like you to personally ensure we see everyone. You're to keep all the men in an orderly line in the servant's dining area. We'll call them one-by-one. And we'll need absolute silence — including no one walking overhead. Everyone is to remain in the dining room and kitchen, or on the top floor. We'll start with the footmen."

When the corridor was clear, Rex escorted Signora Varotti into the butler's office. He pulled a chair close to a line of tubes attached to the wall. Each one was carefully labelled, allowing Rex to quickly identify the one he needed.

The speaking tubes were a relic from the Victorian times, and most had forgotten about their existence. Prudence, a professional information gatherer, had noted them soon after her arrival.

During the car ride the night before, she'd told Dora, "You'd be amazed how much you can overhear, particularly if you have a keen ear."

Dora had immediately thought of Lucia Varotti, whose hearing allowed her to witness the crime.

Rex whistled into the funnel opening at the end of the tube and then lifted it to his ear. A jaunty whistle was the only reply. Rex recognised the tune as one of Dora's favourite songs.

Rex handed the tube to Signora Varotti and then returned to the corridor. The youngest footman stood waiting. Rex instructed him to walk up and down the hall ten times, and then rap once on the butler's office door. After that, he was to pass along the same set of instructions to the next man in line.

Back in the office, the old woman motioned for Rex to join her. She angled the funnel away from her ear and invited Rex to listen with her.

By now, everyone should be in place. It was showtime, and the stage direction was in Prudence's hands.

* * *

Rex closed his eyes and painted a picture of the scene above in his mind. He focused his full being on the faint sounds coming from the speaking tube.

Dora was to crack open the rear-most window so Brandon and the others could listen from outside. Then she'd have lifted the speaking tube, making sure the top remained open. That done, she was to duck behind the thick window drapes.

Rex heard a strange creak.

"La porta," whispered Signora Varotti.

Two sets of footsteps followed the creak of the door, one tread heavier than the other.

Two sets of footsteps followed the creak of the door, one tread heavier than the other. "Sir Francis, I want to thank you for inviting me to enjoy the beauty of your home and grounds," Prudence said. "It has been a most enjoyable and eye-opening stay. Your world is so much larger than mine."

Her voice sounded tinny over the line. It got clearer as she approached Dora's hiding space. Rex imagined her guiding Sir Francis to the chairs nearest the window.

"It has been a pleasure to have you here and you have been most helpful."

"One thing I have learned is that your political position in the government certainly must cause you problems at times. You work so hard to keep everyone happy."

"Yes, that is true. Politics is not for the faint of heart. There is always someone who would like to undermine my authority if not steal my position."

"I don't know how you do it...how you keep yourself safe and keep from losing your mind. If it was me, I am certain there would be days when I would probably want to kill someone."

With a nervous laugh, Sir Francis slowly responded, "Well, I guess I have thought about that option a few times, myself."

Prudence looked him in the eye, "Did you think about it when you killed the piano tuner?

The long stretch of silence had Rex worrying something had gone awry. But when Sir Francis spoke, his voice trembling with emotion, Rex understood the news had simply struck him dumb.

"Why would you suggest such a thing, Prudence?"

"Because of what Miss Laurent told me. She's upstairs. She came to warn me that your arrest is imminent."

"What?" Sir Francis gasped. "That's ridiculous. Theodora promised to clear my name. That's why I asked her to come."

Rex's mouth was painfully dry. This was taking too long. Prudence had revealed her hand, but Sir Francis hadn't taken the bait. Desperation urged him to dash up the stairs and confront the ambassador. But his promise to Signora Varotti's son kept him in place. He'd pledged not to leave her behind.

Prudence's voice recalled Rex's attention.

"Apparently, she wasn't aware of your intentions. She said Lord Clark and Lord Rex intend to hand you over to the Italians. She hinted you'll be in an Italian jail before supper."

"You must come to my defence," Sir Francis begged. "My wife is your cousin. Think of her, if not of me. You must know I'm innocent."

Prudence's voice dropped lower. "I — I cannot. You see, I couldn't sleep that night. I was at the window and saw a shadow on the drive. I know you left that house."

"You couldn't have. All the windows were dark. The curtains were drawn."

Prudence borrowed from Signora Varotti's tale. "I was warm. I was going to open the window. Then I saw you walking away. You had on your coat — the one with your lapel pin on the front. Why did you do it, Sir Francis? What was that woman to you?"

"She was no one," Sir Francis replied in a harsh tone. "She brought up ancient history and made vile threats. I didn't want to hurt her, but she gave me no choice. You see, I'm innocent of murder. It was self-defence!"

A terrifying screech echoed through the line. Then Rex heard Brandon Shaw's voice. Sir Francis's lie must have been too much for the clerk to bear.

"You did it! You killed them both — Donald and Mary. Did you know she was his sister? Why? Why did you murder two good people?"

"To cover up his traitorous actions. Isn't that correct?" Dora asked.

Rex exhaled in relief at the sound of his beloved's voice.

"I was here three years ago. I remember what happened. Donald Tomlins didn't kill himself to avoid prosecution for sharing state secrets, did he? You made him take the fall for your actions. What I don't understand is why you'd be so foolish."

"Because I needed the money!" Sir Francis replied. "How am I to represent our nation on the mere pittance I receive? State secrets? I gave no word of military movements. All I shared was information that might sweeten a deal. Isn't that why I'm here? If the government won't pay me for my work, why shouldn't I take from the local pockets?"

"You are not a dealmaker, Sir Francis. You are a representative of the British people. Your job is to negotiate on their behalf, not sell their private information to the highest bidder."

"Who are you to judge me?" Sir Francis spat. "A foreign grifter, an orphan, and a lowly clerk. It will be your word against mine. The Italians will protect me."

The door banged open, and more footsteps entered the room. "You're wrong," a male voice countered.

Rex recognised it at once. Clark had arrived with the cavalry.

"Arrest the ambassador and confine him to his quarters until transport arrangements can be made."

Rex straightened up from his hunched position. He didn't need to hear the rest to know what would happen next.

Signora Varotti passed him the speaking tube. With unerring aim, she reached up and patted him on his arm. "Tutto è bene ciò che finisce bene."

Rex didn't need Dora's help to translate that line. The title of the famous Shakespearean comedy rang through his mind.

Despite the odds and the foreign soil, they'd solved two murders and achieved justice for the British nation. Furthermore, they'd done so without having to reveal any of their own secrets.

Rex was certain Lord Audley would agree that all's well that ends well, indeed.

Epilogue

D ora and Rex had little time to celebrate solving the
mystery. They were still the Johnnies on the spot and
had responsibility for setting things in Rome to rights.

Dora, Rex, Clark and Prudence came to an agreement on
how much of Sir Francis's misdeeds to report. Prudence
demanded carte blanche. The men threw around phrases like
national security interests and *traitorous behaviour*, demanding
she keep quiet about it all.

As the only unbiased member of the group, it fell to Dora to
negotiate a middle ground. A few days later, Casper Eadmund
published a rare, midweek column, with exclusive coverage of
Sir Francis Cannon's arrest and downfall.

According to Eadmund's sources, Sir Francis had killed his
Italian lover when she threatened to reveal their relationship to
his wife. The Carabinieri gained full credit for their
investigation into the crime, while the British government
would ensure he was punished.

Privately, Lord Audley paid a visit to the Tomlins family.
Reeling from the loss of another child, they had no desire to
see their name in the headlines. Lord Audley promised to

arrange for repatriation of Mary's body, and for Donald's widow to receive a government pension for the remainder of her days.

Poor Clark, still the highest ranking Englishman in Rome, had to remain in the ambassador post until a replacement arrived. As Dora fully expected, he rose to the challenge. The first thing he did was ask Rex's grandmother to act as hostess. Between his charming demeanour and her expert hand, they smoothed things over with Re Vittorio Emanuele and Mussolini. Brandon Shaw stuck by Clark's side, ensuring he never showed up to a meeting unprepared.

When they finally freed themselves of their collective responsibilities, Dora, Rex, Clark, and the rest of their household departed for a well-earned rest on the isle of Capri. Edith, Caledonia, and Prudence left shortly after, travelling back to London together.

It was late summer when Dora turned the knob of her Belgravia home and proclaimed their return. Rex swept her off her feet, carrying her over the threshold and straight up to their room. Inga and Harris made themselves scarce.

A week later, their lives were returning to something that resembled normal, at least by their standards. Casper Eadmund covered their appearance on the social circuit with glee in his Sunday column.

For Dora, being back in London gave her the same cosy feeling as sliding her feet into well-worn slippers. The noted femme fatale, with a passion for travel, discovered the joy of having a place to call home. Although the travel bug would likely soon bite, for now, she was content to kick up her heels in the Big Smoke.

No undercover mission could end without a tête-à-tête with Lord Audley. In a rare exception to their modus operandi, he was coming to them. And in the middle of the afternoon, no less. Dora took full advantage of the rare opportunity to put her feet up and relax.

The grandfather clock chimed the hour. It was four PM and Lord Audley was due at any moment. Dora set her latest read, another of Mrs Christie's novels, aside and shifted her legs. In doing so, she bumped against an unmovable, furry mass.

Mews lay curled against her feet, now staring at her through slitted eyes. She'd been so engrossed in her book she'd failed to note his arrival. It made no difference that she'd sat there first, or that he was uninvited. His low growl threatened retribution should she consider moving again.

Was the little beast showing her affection? Until that moment, the pair had lived a peaceful coexistence that relied entirely on ignoring one another.

But ever since their return from Italy, Mews had softened in his demeanour. He no longer hid under the chair legs and swiped at her ankles when she walked past.

Perhaps it was time for her to do the same.

Slowly, Dora leaned forward with her right hand outstretched. She let her hand hover over the cat's marmalade-coloured head.

Mews lifted his nose into the air and sniffed at her palm.

Dora fought against her instinct to pull away before his claws drew blood. The cat's warm breath skimmed over her palm. It seemed he was equally hesitant to cross this last line that kept them apart.

Dora shifted her hand, angling it the way she'd seen Rex do. Mews stretched his neck and brushed his cheek against her palm.

Rex came into the sitting room and stopped in mid-sentence when he saw his pet lying in Dora's lap, purring contentedly while she stroked his back.

"How? Err, what... but, huh?" was all he mumbled.

Dora's tinkling laugh made the cat open one eye. "It seems he's decided to keep me as well. What was it you were saying?"

The moment broken, the cat leapt down and sauntered off, his tail swishing through the air.

"Lord Audley rang. He is on his way. Would you care to join me in waiting for him in the drawing room?"

Dora rose from the cushioned window seat and brushed the stray hairs from her wide-leg trousers. Then she slid her arm through her husband's and said, "I thought you'd never ask."

Ten minutes later, Harris escorted Lord Audley into the drawing room. Dora was struck by the changes in him. His salt and pepper hair was decidedly more salt than not. A new line marked his wide forehead. The once indomitable man showed signs of being a mere mortal.

Dora didn't like it.

She rushed over, latched onto his shoulders, and kissed him on each cheek. "That was from Nonna Matilda. She sends her love and promises to make you a tiramisu the next time you visit."

"I'll give our new ambassador a few months to settle into the role before I turn up. But mayhap Christmas in Rome can be in the cards." Lord Audley peered at her through a hooded gaze. "That is, if you two can manage to behave yourselves until then."

"We shall do our best," Rex pledged, offering him a hand.

Dora stepped clear to allow the men to shake. She tapped her chin. "You've gone too far, Rex darling. Lord Audley isn't fool enough to believe such a promise. You should have said we'll take the matter into consideration."

"I've known you too long to believe either of those statements."

Dora pretended to be offended, but ruined it by laughing. "Please, sit. Tell us what has happened since we last spoke."

Lord Audley chose the wide armchair that Inga preferred. Rex and Dora lounged across from him on the new leather sofa they'd purchased in Italy.

The spy master sighed heavily.

"Has it been that bad?" Dora asked.

"Discovering our ambassador is a double murderer is hardly a walk in the park. Worse yet was having to break the news to the Tomlins family." He wiped his hand over his mouth. "At least now they know who was responsible for ending Donald's life."

Dora's eyes shimmered with emotion. "Inga and I paid a visit to his grave before we left Rome. It was the least we could do, although it didn't make a dent in our guilt. If we'd worked faster, or looked harder at Sir Francis during our first visit to Rome, perhaps both Donald and Mary would still be alive."

"You did the best you could in a difficult situation," Lord Audley reminded her. "Sir Francis is the ultimate one to blame. For that, he will spend the rest of his days behind bars."

"What of his wife, Lady Emily?" Rex asked, moving the conversation onto safer ground.

"As you'd expect, the courts granted her a divorce. She's staying with Queen Mary for the time being. Hopefully, in due time, she'll find the strength to return to society." Lord Audley leaned forward. "What of Miss Adams? Is she truly Casper Eadmund?"

"Ah, so Edith shared the secret with you?" Dora replied. "We were shocked, as well. Don't worry. We were very careful around her. If she'd caught even a whiff of the truth of my identity or our purpose in Italy, we'd have handled things very differently."

"I'll keep an eye on her," Audley offered. "She must have access to a vast treasury of gossip. Who knows? We may find use for her in the future."

"Speaking of the future," Rex said, cutting in. "There is one matter we wish to discuss with you."

Lord Audley's fingers tightened on the armrests, but his voice didn't betray his nerves. "I suppose it was inevitable. With the changes in your relationship, you'd envision other pathways..."

"No. You misunderstand." Rex huffed in annoyance with himself.

"We're as committed to the cause as ever," Dora said, taking control of the conversation. "And that is why we took stock of our companions. We've been ever so lucky to have Inga and Harris, the twins, and their sister Cynthia to support our endeavours. But there's also been someone else who has stood by our side, through thick and thin."

Lord Audley scrunched his brow, adding more wrinkles to bracket the new line. "Do you mean the Dowager Duchess?"

"It's Clark. Lord Clark," Rex corrected. "I know he seems the last person you'd want on a secret assignment, but we can't deny his use. Have you ever considered — would you consider adding him to our team?"

Lord Audley's eyes opened wide, betraying his surprise.

But he didn't say no. He didn't say anything at all. Dora took his silence as positive.

Rex filled the gap. "There's no need to answer right away. We're not suggesting he train to be a spy, although I'm sure he'd be capable."

Lord Audley steepled his fingers. "What did you have in mind?"

"Rex and I can handle the spying, but there's the pesky matter of murders that dog our footsteps. Often, we need someone to provide misdirection while we sleuth, or an extra pair of hands with the investigations. Clark is well-connected and well-known for his outlandish antics. As far as cover stories go, I've seen much worse."

"I must say that I haven't given Lord Clark much thought, but there is some validity in your suggestion. Let's not rush into anything. Should the right time and case arise, we can discuss the matter further. Is that satisfactory?"

Dora glanced at Rex. He'd been the one to raise the idea with her. If he wanted to push for approval, she'd stand at his side.

Rex released his breath and grinned. "It's more than I expected, so I will accept your response."

Dora lifted a thick envelope from the table and handed it to her mentor. "We compiled a dossier on Mussolini, as you asked. Inga was kind enough to type everything up, so you don't have to struggle with our handwriting. Unless you need something else from us regarding the Italians, I'd say we're free to take on our next assignment."

Lord Audley's eyes flicked left before his gaze returned to Dora's face. Something had crossed his mind, but he didn't say it. "Nothing for the moment. Best you return to the party scene and uphold your reputation as Bright Young Things, especially since Prudence Adams has her eye on you."

"Are you sure there's nothing else..." Dora gave Lord Audley a hard look. He was hiding a secret. She was sure of it. "We can throw our clothes back into our cases and depart again, if you need."

The man waved off the idea. "Not every problem is for you to solve, Dora. Now, I should be on my way. Social calls are meant to be brief, and we don't want chins to wag."

He left as quickly as he'd arrived, without a backward glance. Dora suspected that the new furrow in his brow was still in place.

Rex wrapped his arms around her and went to kiss her, but stopped at her expression.

"Oh no. There's that look. What are you plotting, bride of mine?"

"Who, me?" Dora replied, fluttering her lashes. "I haven't the faintest what you mean."

Rex let it slide, but only because he knew she'd eventually come clean. And she would, as soon as she had a plan in place.

Lord Audley carried a burden. Anything worrying him was worth her attention. If she wanted to uncover the root of his problems, she had to call in the biggest weapon in her arsenal.

She gave her husband a peck on the lips and then pulled free from his embrace.

"Where are you going?" he asked.

"To ring your grandmother. She offered to host a luncheon to celebrate our return with our families. I want to add one more name to her guest list."

* * *

Want more Dora and Rex? They will be back in **The Cryptic Cold Case**.

Can Dora and Rex solve this cold case without ending up in hot water?

London, 1923. In a Mayfair dining room, Theodora Laurent and Lord Rex Bankes-Fernsby make an incredible discovery. Rex's sister Caledonia is a naturally gifted codebreaker.

Upon hearing this news, Lord Audley, London's spy master, asks for their help with a most unusual mission.

Twenty-five years ago, his wife died in a riding accident.

Recently, he learned her death may not have been an accident. In search of the truth, he discovered cryptic messages hidden away in her old things.

With Caledonia's help, Dora and Rex delve into the mysterious case of Lady Audley. Each decoded message reveals a tantalising clue. But, in the excitement of the chase, they forget one fact.

They aren't the only ones who know what those messages say.

The closer they get to the truth, the harder the killer will work to keep his misdeeds buried in the past.

Find out in **The Cryptic Cold Case**. Order your copy now on Amazon.

Want to keep updated on my newest books? Subscribe to my newsletter for book news, sales, special offers, and great reading recommendations. You can sign up here: lynnmorrison. myflodesk.com/dcd-newsletter

Historical Notes

In the summer of 2023, my husband insisted we visit Il Vittoriale degli Italiani during a trip to Lake Garda. He explained it had been the home of Gabriele D'Annuzio and was a must-see for our half-Italian children.

Despite having studied Italian and lived in Italy, I had to admit I wasn't familiar with the place or its previous owner. After my husband got over his shock, he handed me the assignment to remedy my intellectual failing. A skim read of the relevant Wikipedia pages did not adequately prepare me for the experience.

D'Annuzio was a much beloved literary genius of his day. He was also eccentric. His home included two different reception rooms — one for people he liked and another for those he didn't. He once kept Mussolini waiting for hours.

His bathroom had over two thousand items in it. I'm not sure that soap and a toothbrush were on that list. I found his lying-in-state room to be particularly gruesome, because he designed and built it years before his death.

Of greater interest to me was the story about the inter-war

time period. Through the tour of his home, his museum, and the house grounds, I discovered more about post-WWI Italy.

Most often, when we think of Italy and the world wars, our minds go to their role as antagonist in the second war. History, however, is rarely so simple. Italy fought alongside England, France, and the United States in WWI. Millions of Italians died in battle. Even now, a century later, there are still signs marking the rivers that flowed with death and blood.

Yet, when it came time to divide the spoils, Italy was pushed to the side. Promises went unfulfilled. The Italians, who'd sacrificed so much, came away with too little. D'Annuzio referred to peace as a 'mutilated victory'. The bitter taste opened space for men like D'Annuzio and Mussolini to foster a nationalistic spirit. Although those two ended up on opposite sides of the matter by the end, in the early days, they raised their voices together to inspire the Italians to rise above world expectations and reclaim their place as a superpower to be admired and feared.

Mussolini invested heavily in the industrialisation of Italy during the inter-war period. My descriptions of the factories on the periphery of Rome reflect the changes that took place across the country. While many countries suffered during the depression of the 1930s, Italy experienced growth. Unfortunately, Mussolini's choice to ally himself with Hitler destroyed the positives changes he'd overseen.

With so much focus on Hitler's rise to power, and rightfully so, we often forget just how early Mussolini came onto the world stage, making Italy the first Fascist state. England eyed the Italian Prime Minister and his ideas with worry. While the Germans suffered from poverty, the Italians had a navy capable of causing significant disruption to shipping lines.

I can well imagine someone like Lord Audley wanting to know more about this Mussolini and his plans. If a British spy went undercover among the Italian elite, Gabriele D'Annuzio's home would have been an ideal place to visit. Outspoken, opinionated, and untouchable due to his beloved status as war hero and poetic genius, he was a fount of information.

And so, my story began there, on the shores of the freshwater Lago di Garda, with Dora smiling at his side.

My choice of Scaligero Castle as the opening setting came through a twist of fate. During our family visit to Sirmione, I paused to read a sign about renovations to the castle. When I spotted dates in the early 1920s, I grabbed my phone and began snapping pictures.

Similarly, our trip to Rome offered me the chance to crisscross the city on foot, as I had my characters do. I did not, however, tour the tunnels beneath the Colosseum. The locations of the ambassador's villa and Nonna Matilda's home are purely products of my imagination.

Here are two sources you can consult if you'd like more information:

Gomellini, Matteo, and Gianni Toniolo, 'The Industrialization of Italy, 1861–1971', in Kevin Hjortshøj O'Rourke, and Jeffrey Gale Williamson (eds), The Spread of Modern Industry to the Periphery since 1871 (Oxford, 2017; online edn, Oxford Academic, 23 Mar. 2017)

Il Vittoriale: https://www.vittoriale.it/en

Acknowledgments

Thanks to Ken Morrison and Anne Radcliffe for helping me wrangle this plot into a proper story. I especially appreciated their patient guidance when two different characters went off the rails.

Thanks to Brenda Chapman and Ewa Bartnik for beta reading. They provided great feedback and caught many errors. Additional thanks to Lois King, Anne Kavcic, Monica Cobine, and Heidi Langan for identifying the last few typos.

To all my readers who connect with me, either in my Facebook reader group or via email, your support means the world to me. I love watching our community of readers grow.

Acknowledgements

The Cryptic Cold Case
A Dora and Rex 1920s Mystery

Can Dora and Rex solve this cold case without ending up in hot water?

London, 1923. In a Mayfair dining room, Theodora Laurent and Lord Rex Bankes-Fernsby make an incredible discovery. Rex's sister Caledonia is a naturally gifted codebreaker.

Upon hearing this news, Lord Audley, London's spy master, asks for their help with a most unusual mission.

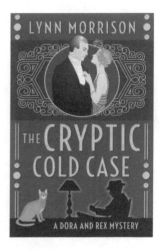

Twenty-five years ago, his wife died in a riding accident. Recently, he learned her death may not have been an accident. In search of the truth, he discovered cryptic messages hidden away in her old things.

With Caledonia's help, Dora and Rex delve into the mysterious case of Lady Audley. Each decoded message reveals a tantalising clue. But, in the excitement of the chase, they forget one fact.

They aren't the only ones who know what those messages say.

The closer they get to the truth, the harder the killer will work to keep his misdeeds buried in the past.

The Cryptic Cold Case will be out April 2024. Order your copy now.

About the Author

Lynn Morrison lives in Oxford, England along with her husband, two daughters and two cats. Born and raised in Mississippi, her wanderlust attitude has led her to live in California, Italy, France, the UK, and the Netherlands. Despite having rubbed shoulders with presidential candidates and members of parliament, night-clubbed in Geneva and Prague, explored Japanese temples and scrambled through Roman ruins, Lynn's real life adventures can't compete with the stories in her mind.

She is as passionate about reading as she is writing, and can almost always be found with a book in hand. You can find out more about her on her website LynnMorrisonWriter.com.

You can chat with her directly in her Facebook group - Lynn Morrison's Not a Book Club - where she talks about books, life and anything else that crosses her mind.

facebook.com/nomadmomdiary

instagram.com/nomadmomdiary

bookbub.com/authors/lynn-morrison

goodreads.com/nomadmomdiary

amazon.com/Lynn-Morrison/e/B00IKC1LVW

Also by Lynn Morrison

Raven's Joy

Raven's Matriarch

Raven's Storm

<u>Wandering Witch Urban Fantasy</u>

A Queen Only Lives Twice

Made in United States
Troutdale, OR
08/16/2024

22064603R00148